◆◆◆◆◆◆

ALSO BY
Mildred Houghton Comfort

WINTER *on the*
JOHNNY SMOKER

SEARCH THROUGH
PIRATE'S ALLEY

◆◆◆◆◆◆

TREASURE
on the
JOHNNY SMOKER

MILDRED HOUGHTON COMFORT

Illustrated by James MacDonald

J

WILLIAM MORROW & COMPANY
NEW YORK, 1947

* fl *

TABLE of CONTENTS

❖❖❖❖❖❖

TREASURE
on the
JOHNNY SMOKER

❖❖❖❖❖❖

CHAPTER 1.

The House on the Hill

❖❖❖❖❖❖❖❖❖❖❖❖❖

MARY AND RELLA, the little Dustin girls, stood amid a tangle of goldenrod and looked down over Reads Landing into the hazy Indian summer distance. In the fall of 1875, Reads Landing was as lively a village as any in Minnesota. Lying at the foot of Lake Pepin, which was not really a lake but a vast widening of the Mississippi, the settlement in its crescent of hills reverberated to the staccato call of the Chippewa boats or the booming of the river packets.

But the two girls did not even see the great river today. Instead, they were watching the Wabasha road, shading their eyes with their hands, looking for Timothy. He had gone to the mill to get some shingles for Billy. It was a mile and a half walk, but Timothy always made the distance in record time. At any moment he would appear at the turn of the road.

Billy, his long back bent over his task of fastening muskrat skins to shingles, sat on the battered old bench where he always did his work. All about him were curls of the trimmed shingles. He worked with meticulous care, shaping a shingle to a point at one end, then drawing the skin, fur-side in, over the wood, tacking the tiny head to the top of the point and pulling out the paws. Always the fluffy tail dangled.

There were around sixty skins hanging in the woodshed to dry, golden-brown and gray skins of a thickness seldom found in Minnesota.

The pile of skins at Billy's feet had just been dropped off by Indian Joe on one of his regular trips. The fresh blueberry pie that Mrs. Dustin had baked for the noon meal had, as usual, worked its magic, for Indian Joe, anticipating a treat, invariably gave the Dustins first choice of his pelts.

As he checked the handsome furs after Indian Joe had departed, Billy glanced up to see his mother in the kitchen doorway. Tall and almost majestic in her voluminous skirt with the tight basque, she came down the back steps with a rustle of freshly ironed blue and white calico. She appraised the furry brown skins with an expert and critical eye.

"Pretty good haul?" Billy inquired, handing her a particularly handsome pelt. "Pretty good trade? We'd never have gotten them at market price without the help of that blueberry pie."

"You wouldn't have had the blueberry pie if Rella and I hadn't picked the blueberries in the summer,"

Mary boasted, tossing her thin, brown braids and wrinkling her small, pert nose. "I discovered the patch: it was like a pale blue carpet, the berries were so thick."

"And I learned how to keep them fresh," Rella added. "Didn't I, Mama? That Indian half-breed said if we kept them in cold water and changed the water every few days, we'd have fresh berries in January."

"Not at the rate I make pies," Mrs. Dustin remarked dryly. "I had that blueberry pie ready for dinner, but I guess we can make shift with apple sauce."

"Oh, Mother!" Four young voices protested, for Timothy had appeared just in time to hear the decision. In his arms were two large bundles of new shingles, his blue eyes and the top of his dark head visible over his load.

It was Timothy who said, in that persuasive voice of his, "Listen, Mama. I was down at the river, and some of the men think the *Johnny Smoker* might be in today. Father would be mightily disappointed if he didn't get his blueberry pie for the first dinner after he comes back."

It was a big event for all the Dustins when the *Johnny Smoker* came in. Captain Dustin had purchased the little side-wheeler the year before, and had already made a good many paying trips up and down the river. The whole family always waited eagerly for news of the latest trip. And when the Captain, with his ready laugh and his twinkling blue eyes, was at home, all the children, from nineteen-year-old Billy to Rella, the youngest, felt that the white house on the hill came to life.

"Oh, Timothy," Rella exclaimed. "I almost forgot to tell you. A boy came to see you this morning. He came to the front door while Mama had her hands in the bread dough, and I answered."

"What did he want?" asked Timothy.

"He said he wanted to go on a three-day hunting trip, for ducks. He said you had been recommended to him as a trapper and hunter, and he wanted to know if you would go with him. He had already bought supplies. His name is Henri Derosia and he's staying at the Union House. He wants you to meet him there at dawn."

"How many days did he say?"

"Three, he thought," Rella answered. "He said he had heard at the Union House that the *Johnny Smoker* wouldn't be in for about three days. When she does come in, he's taking her to Prairie du Chien, if Father will accept him as a passenger."

"Sh!" Timothy warned, but his mother had heard.

"So the *Johnny Smoker* might be in this morning, before noon?" she asked, her hands on her hips.

J. MAC DONALD

"Make a blueberry pie because Father might be coming in and be disappointed?"

Timothy grinned impishly.

"Father wouldn't be nearly as disappointed as I would be, if I didn't have blueberry pie for dinner. Do I have to be a captain before I get blueberry pie?"

Isabel, the oldest Dustin girl, came to the doorway of the kitchen.

"You have the appetite of a roustabout, Timothy," she teased. "But don't worry. I already have a blueberry pie in the oven and dinner's ready."

Timothy sniffed the clean smell of the house as they all went in. Mrs. Dustin was one of those Reads Landing housekeepers who believed in both fall and spring cleaning. Fresh straw lay thickly beneath the tightly stretched new rag rug in the sitting room.

"Like walking on thick pine needles or moss," Timothy observed.

The white lace curtains had been stiffly starched and tied back with carefully ironed ribbons. On the arms and backs of the chairs Isabel had deftly tacked new antimacassars. She made her own patterns, borrowed from the intricate designs of snowflakes and spring flowers.

"Too nice to lean back against," Timothy mused. "Anyway, I won't sit back until I've washed my hair."

Mrs. Dustin was pleased. Of her three menfolk Timothy had the greatest love of beauty.

◇◇◇◇◇◇◇
◇◇◇◇◇◇◇

Before dawn the following morning, Isabel knocked on Timothy's door, went in, and shook him gently awake. He was snuggled in his featherbed, comforters up to his chin, and there was frost across the braided rug where his damp boots lay.

"Mornin' in the swamp!" Isabel whispered. "Ducks against the moon! Get up, voyageur, and I'll soon have breakfast ready."

She had a pot of coffee on the back of the stove, simmering, and a stack of buckwheat cakes on the stove hearth when Timothy came downstairs, his eyes heavy-lidded.

"Wash at the back door," she suggested. "Basin's on the bench beside the pail of rain water."

Timothy made short shrift of his ablutions. Although there was no ice in the water in the pail, there was liquid ice, he would have sworn, in the basin into which he plunged his hands to splash his face.

Early as it was, there were little squares of gold light in many windows of the gray town, and down the road swung a lighted lantern. The man carrying it was a fantastic shadow against the dark woods.

Down the Mississippi, in front of the landing, came a big, dark raft. The men who had rowed it were bringing it into the shore, probably just long enough for a few drinks and to take on fuel and provisions. Lights shone in the wannagan, and voices floated up, clear and strong.

"Logs!" Timothy said to himself. "That raft came down the St. Croix and through Lake Pepin, no doubt about it. The pilot's Marcel de Prieu. I'd know that voice anywhere."

The musical cadence of Marcel's commands echoed up into the bowl of hills.

"*Yip*, in front!" At this order the five men at the forward end of the raft lifted their heavy oars above their heads, thrusting the long blades deeply into the water, and walked across the string. Then they turned and walked back to their stations as the men at the other end took up their oars at the call, "*Yip*, behind!"

Timothy hurried into the kitchen.

"Don't fry any more cakes for me, Isabel." He rushed about, picking up his wraps. "I'll have mine on the wannagan. Five strings on that raft, with the wannagan in the middle. Al Cronk's cook shanty, I betcha. He can make flapjacks as big as dinner plates!"

"You'd better eat your breakfast at home," Mrs. Dustin suggested as she came into the kitchen.

"Aw, Maw," Timothy objected. "Will and Gene Crocker eat on the wannagans all the time."

"Their mother doesn't like to cook." Mrs. Dustin was short.

"You're a fine cook, Maw," Timothy acknowledged, "but a change is good for anybody."

"Grease and blackstrap instead of butter and maple syrup would be a change, all right," Mrs. Dustin agreed. "Just the same, you eat your breakfast at home. If you want grease with your cakes, Isabel will heat some for you."

Timothy sat down at the table. He bolted his cakes almost as fast as his dog, Shep, who had already gobbled the food Isabel had set out for him.

"Well," Timothy said, "I'll start Henri Derosia on his hunting career in Smith's Slough and be back at Sanborn's Point on the third day. All right?"

"Better take some molasses cookies with you," Mrs. Dustin advised. "And take care of yourself, son. Be careful of that gun."

Timothy waited impatiently while his mother packed the cookies, then kissed her good-by.

"Have I ever been careless?" he asked with his winning smile.

"Not you," his mother admitted. "But you don't know about this other boy."

He walked away from the house with the easy swing of the forest-born, calling back consolation to his yelping dog. He felt very grown-up to be out with the early birds.

CHAPTER 2.

The Hunting Trip

◆◆◆◆◆◆◆◆◆◆◆◆◆◆◆

ON THE SAINT PAUL ROAD, that wound from the top of the bluff above the Dustin house to the lower road, Timothy stepped aside to let the stagecoach rumble by. A few minutes later the boardwalk in the town resounded to his vigorous stride.

In the Union House he inquired at the desk for Henri Derosia. The sleepy clerk, tiredly rubbing his bald spot, mumbled, "You wake him, Timothy. I'm plumb tuckered."

But Henri was already awake, and the Llewellyn setter, that had been sleeping on the braided rug beside his bed, accepted Timothy's advances gingerly, retreating after each overture to her young master, who was lacing his boots.

"A one-man dog," Henri boasted. "That's the nicest thing about a highbred dog—any dog maybe. You give her a bone, and she gives you a lifetime of devotion. Eh, Queenie?"

Queenie looked at her master with soulful eyes.

The equipment that Henri Derosia had assembled was more than adequate. When the two boys had carried it to the river, Timothy put much of the food in his own canoe, feeling that he was less liable to ship water than the inexperienced Henri.

But Henri was surprisingly deft with the paddle, amazingly confident when the canoes hit the current and were caught for a moment in the pull, and perfectly sure of his technique as he swung his canoe in behind Timothy's at the bank of willows leading into the Wisconsin sloughs.

"He'll teach me a thing or two," Timothy decided. "He doesn't need a guide; all he wanted was company." It was beautiful to watch the way Henri's wrist turned the paddle, never once lifting it out of the water but sliding it close to the curve of the canoe with a motion that was like a caress.

The narrow waterways were frosty, but a few bright scarlet shrubs remained in sheltered coves, and some scrub cottonwoods showered golden leaves. The light wind made little rustlings in the tops of poplars, even when they were not tall. Always they whispered, like neighbors talking together.

Timothy set up the pup tent that first night in a sheltered swale, but the ground was so damp it felt cold even through the Hudson's Bay blankets. He built a small fire at the entrance to the pup tent, intending to rouse himself, as Billy would have done, each time the fire died down. But he fell asleep almost as soon as he had crawled into the blankets beside Henri, and woke only when the impatient Queenie climbed over him to nose her master. On the second night, a night of cold, glittering stars, he crossed to the hillside, cut some pine boughs, and wove them into a mattress, as Billy had taught him to do. There was frost on the blankets, but he and Henri were warm. "Warm as toast," said Henri.

Timothy soon found that his help was needed—needed badly. Henri could not shoot. Although Timothy tried to be patient, he could not understand Henri's awkwardness with a gun. The Dustins were all marksmen, even the girls. But Henri was not careless. Even Mrs. Dustin could not have accused him of that.

Timothy's voice was actually hoarse that third day. He kept shouting, "When Queenie flushes the birds up, swing your gun in the direction they are flying. Don't wait until they are way up in the sky. When you see them flying west, for instance, fire in front of them. They'll fly *into* your fire."

But Henri seemed never to learn. He was profusely apologetic.

"I can't focus them in time," he explained. "I never miss a target. I can always hit a bull's-eye. But live partridges and live ducks move too fast. And I can never guess which way they are going to move."

"They move in a beautiful curve," Timothy

pointed out. "You'd think to hear you that they zigzagged."

The day wore on.

"I guess it takes time to learn anything," Timothy decided. "Even Queenie looks discouraged. She fairly sags every time you miss."

The ducks continued to fly, usually in a V formation, but sometimes whole flocks descended to enjoy the wild rice in the bottoms. On the hillside, partridges burred up out of the bushes. A cock pheasant, with his sudden rush of wings, almost brushed Henri's arm. He fled through the brush, a vivid splash of shining color.

On the last day, when it was almost dusk and time to start back across the river to Sanborn's Point, just above Reads Landing, Timothy decided to take some game home. Up until then he had given Henri all the good chances.

"I'll watch you," Henri offered wearily. "No use in my wasting any more ammunition."

The crackle of Timothy's gun brought ducks spiraling down into the water while the rest of the birds fled with a wild quacking. Where it was shallow, Timothy waded out to retrieve the ducks he had shot. Where it was deeper, Queenie went. But Queenie's heart was not in her work. She nosed her master each time, as if to say, "What's the matter with *you? Do* something."

When Timothy had all the ducks they could use, the boys cooked the last meal of their trip, frying the remaining bacon in a skillet and sliding in the last few eggs. Henri was toasting the dry bread on a stick before the fire when Timothy whispered, "Look! Don't turn around. Just look sidewise towards the canoes."

Henri looked. Queenie, the one-man dog, was nervously transferring the ducks from Timothy's canoe to her master's. She moved quietly, fearfully, but she moved purposefully.

"That's all right," Timothy said with a short laugh. "Look out! Your toast is catching on fire."

"You see," Henri said ruefully, "even my dog apologizes for me."

The boys tipped up the empty canoe as a windbreak and sat under the curve of the low roof eating their supper. Queenie came and lay close to Henri, lifting her soulful eyes to him and wagging her tail.

When the boys began to pack up again, Queenie dashed about with Timothy in friendly fashion. It was as if she forgave him for his expert marksmanship, now that she herself had righted things.

"Queenie," said Timothy, "you're my idea of a good dog, one that tries to cover up her master's faults. But we'll teach Henri, believe me."

The two canoes slid out of Smith's Slough, and

Henri and Timothy paddled back across the broad Mississippi. They drew their canoes up on the yellow sand, and climbed to a high embankment from which they watched the water take on the glorious hues of sunset. Here the Mississippi widened to become Lake Pepin, and the great river was broader here than at any other point along its hundreds of miles to the sea.

A silence grew between the boys as they sat down to rest before making the last two miles to Reads Landing.

The silence was broken by the low, long-drawn-out, melodious whistle of a boat, a whistle that echoed back from the high, rocky bluffs.

"The *Johnny Smoker!*" Timothy shouted. "The *Johnny Smoker!*"

Henri, still dreamily aware of the mingled scents of damp leaves, sumac, and juniper, and the sounds of ducks far off and rustlings of little animals near by, got slowly to his feet. He saw, plowing through a sea of rose fire shot through with blue haze, a small side-wheeler, a red light on one smokestack, a green light on the other. The sturdy little boat was making twin wakes of pink and white foam.

"So that's the *Johnny Smoker.*" Henri appraised it. "I've ridden on the *Muscatine* and the *Savannah*. It will be fun trying this. I'm hoping to make my return trip to Prairie du Chien on board her. Who runs her?"

"My father," Timothy answered proudly. "My father's both owner and captain. He's the pilot too. He bought the boat about a year ago. My family and Johnny Sterling lived on it all last winter. It was frozen into a cove where we cut timber."

"Must have been jolly," Henri said. "Who's Johnny Sterling?"

"He's a friend of the family and now he's first mate on the *Johnny Smoker*," Timothy explained. "Last spring we were the first to get through the ice and we won the race the river boats have every spring from here to St. Paul. That meant a prize and some nice freight jobs. Johnny Sterling was a big help when we won that race."

"The *Johnny Smoker* carries cargo?" asked Henri.

"Sure," said Timothy. "Apples, nuts, sugar, flour, coffee—everything."

"Does she carry furs?"

"She'll carry furs if they happen to be in the freight billings. But come on," Timothy added. "We must go if we're to reach the Landing by the time she docks."

CHAPTER 3.

Timothy's Man-Sized Job

◆◆◆◆◆◆◆◆◆◆◆◆◆◆◆◆◆

CAPTAIN WILLIAM DUSTIN, tall, broad, and vigorous, came out of the pilothouse and down the steps to the gangplank of the *Johnny Smoker*. He waited until a roustabout picked up the heavy coiled rope that lay on the bow, jumped off before the boat touched the shore, and fastened the rope about one of the posts on the levee.

The Captain waved to the familiar crowd that always met his boat, and his chin whiskers lifted to a jaunty angle, while his old meerschaum pipe puffed clouds of white smoke into the still November air.

Rella and Mary were waiting in the crowd, and he singled them out with a smile and a wave of the hand. Behind him came Johnny Sterling, tall, lithe, and slim, peering around the Captain's broad back.

Timothy and Henri were beaching their canoes and soon joined the family group.

Mrs. Dustin and Isabel were waiting at the door of the house to welcome them all as they climbed the hill in record time. After a joyful greeting, they seated them at the table to enjoy a savory supper. Henri had been invited to stay, since supper would probably be over at the Union House.

It was a merry group that filled the long oval table.

Isabel and her mother brought in from the kitchen platters of beefsteak, mashed potatoes, and rutabagas. The Captain's favorite coleslaw was flanked by a quivering mound of currant jelly and a dish of pickled crab apples.

Henri Derosia was a delightful guest. He told the story of Queenie's transfer of the ducks, and Mary and Rella both left the table to pat the dog that lay near her master's chair.

When Isabel was serving the thick wedges of apple pie, the Captain brought out packages for his wife from his voluminous pockets, and then tossed a sack of candy on the table. With shrieks of delight Mary and Rella delved into it.

"Well, Mother," said the Captain, "we're pulling out for Prairie du Chien in the morning. Short trip. I'm taking Timothy along this time—for experience."

"Will you take me on as a passenger, sir?" Henri inquired. "My family is living in the Dousman House in Prairie du Chien and they thought I could return there on the *Johnny Smoker*. That's why I remained over instead of taking the stage."

"Guess we can accommodate you, son," the Cap-

tain said with a twinkle in his bright blue eyes. "If
we haven't a stateroom, we can put you in the hold."

And now details were arranged. When Timothy
realized that he was to substitute for Johnny Sterling on this trip, his pride rose to new heights.

"Will I be a mate?" he inquired.

"You may name your own job, Timothy," his
father answered. "But it will be a tough job at first.
Firing! If you want to give a fancy name to stoking
a greedy furnace with cordwood and slabs, it's all
right with me. I'm leaving Johnny here with Billy,
to get the freight ready at the Landing for the next
trip to St. Louis."

Henri went back to the Union House, but Johnny
Sterling stayed on at the Dustin home, for he had
become practically a member of the family since his
winter spent with them on the *Johnny Smoker*.

In the morning Rella was up early enough to walk
down to the boat with her father. One hand was
in his, one in Timothy's, as the three hurried down
the hill over the frosty ground.

"Do hurry on this trip, Father," Rella urged. "It
will be so much nicer when the season's over and
you're home. We're already drying kinnikinnick and
scraping the nice red bark so you'll have tobacco to
smoke in the winter."

"Drying kinnikinnick so I'll have *tobacco* to
smoke!" The Captain laughed lustily. "Johnny Ster-

ling's getting me some Kentucky tobacco, and I mean tobacco. To please your mother, I'll mix it with a little kinnikinnick."

"Father, you've never smoked real tobacco," Rella reminded him. "Maybe you'll have to learn to like it."

"I'll make a prodigious effort," the Captain decided.

Rella waved Timothy on board. She saw him disappear below, as Henri went on deck and followed the Captain to the pilothouse.

Soon the *Johnny Smoker* was chugging along over the misty, cold river, and Timothy kept busy lifting cordwood into the fiery maw of the engine. The cordwood was soon used up and the engine room held mostly slabs. Slabs burned much faster than cordwood and with a great deal more soot.

A roustabout came to relieve Timothy from time to time. Once he said, "Yer own mother wouldn't be knowin' you."

But Timothy had no time to examine his face in a mirror. Whenever the roustabout "spelled" him, he lay down on a bunk and rested.

It was dusk by the time the boat reached Prairie du Chien. Timothy went out on deck to watch the unloading. Henri Derosia had already gone ashore. Expectant merchants, coming on board to see what the Captain had brought them, indulged in much roisterous, rumbling laughter. Captain Dustin's voice was shouting orders. "Step lively! Men, get these barrels of flour into the warehouse before it snows. Have that hardware company send a dray for these stoves. Timothy!"

"Yes, sir," Timothy shouted up.

"Get those bills of lading from my desk in the cabin."

As Timothy started to obey, he heard his father say to someone: "No! Don't take those two packages. Timothy will attend to them. They're insured."

When Timothy came back with the bills, a sturdy old gentleman was standing on the dock with his own clerks. "Get those boxes into our warehouse before closing time," he shouted. "No! Get out of my way, Jake. Can't use you. Don't come on board. The Captain has no use for the likes of you, either. Out of my way!"

Timothy saw that a thin, dark boy, his hat pulled over his eyes, was blocking the gangplank in front of the old gentleman. He backed away, slouched over to some pilings, and mumbled something in a low growl. A stevedore, rolling barrels down the gangplank, almost collided with the fellow, who let out an oath at him.

The tramp of feet, the hustle and bustle, and the loud shouts died away as men and wagons moved off towards the town warehouses. Captain Dustin stood in front of the pilot house, quietly smoking his pipe. Timothy stood beside him.

"Made good time," said the Captain.

"Thanks to me," said Timothy.

"Oh, it's you." Captain Dustin pretended surprise. "I knew you by your voice. That face could stand a washing. Anyway, dip your hands in a basin before you handle these packages I've got in the cabin for you. Too valuable to keep in the hold. They're insured."

Timothy followed his father into the cabin where he washed his hands. He saw, on the table, two immense white boxes, carefully tied. They had all the earmarks of something very special.

"May be nothing more than some fancy food," the Captain said dryly. "Insured because somebody's hankering for it. Most of the Derosia house parties are pretty elaborate, with stuff shipped from as far as Chicago or St. Louis. I want you to deliver these two boxes to Mr. Derosia at the Dousman house. You'll not mistake it," the Captain said and pointed out the path. "When you've done your errand, come straight back and I'll have supper ready for you in the cabin here. The men are in Prairie du Chien. I've given them the evening off."

Timothy raised his chin with a gesture much like his father's. He knew that the Captain liked to cook once in a while, but he also knew that he was being given a rare treat, to dine with him alone. He was being treated like a grown man.

He picked up the two white boxes and made his way down the gangplank. He would wash his face and make himself tidy for the Captain's supper as soon as he had delivered the packages. Men were still disappearing into the dusk, and carts and wagons were rumbling off down the roads. He followed the path his father had indicated and soon saw the Dousman house some distance ahead. It was a large house, and it was brightly lighted throughout.

He had gone only a short way along the path when he became aware that there was someone behind him. His forest-keen ears caught the pad-pad of moccasin-clad feet. He whirled about—but the path was empty.

Suddenly Timothy felt cold. It had never occurred to him that he might be in danger. In Reads Landing nobody ever locked a door, and though the rivermen got drunk they were seldom dangerous. But Timothy did not like the idea of being stalked, even though the person might be merely curious.

He walked faster. Before him there appeared a copse of evergreen shrub. An inner sense told him that someone was lurking there. Still he kept on, gripping the boxes so tightly that his knuckles showed white. There was no wind as there had been earlier in the evening. Cold had settled, still and biting.

As though he were in a nightmare, he saw a crouching figure step suddenly out of the bushes into the path ahead. He stopped dead still with a terrible awareness. The figure came on toward him, and Timothy realized that the fellow was Jake, the thin, dark boy that his father's customer had refused to allow on the boat. He saw Jake's intentions, to trip him and take the boxes. With calm deliberation Timothy set the boxes on the top of the hedge as though to rest himself.

"Hand 'em over," Jake shouted.

"No!" Timothy shouted back. "And get out of my way!"

"You're a nervy little shrimp," the fellow sneered, and reached for the boxes.

But Timothy was quicker than that deliberate reach. He dived, caught Jake by the ankles, and sent him sprawling. Then he backed away, waiting for him to rise. When he was on his feet, Timothy sent a right uppercut to his jaw. Billy had taught him that. The fellow howled, and a smaller boy rushed in from behind Timothy, grabbed him, and pinned his arms down. It was only the suddenness of the attack that enabled the younger boy to get a hold.

"Hang on to him, Zizzy!" Jake yowled.

Timothy shook the boy called Zizzy off like a collie shaking a rag. But, in the meantime, Jake had heaved himself up and seized the two boxes.

Timothy's fury mounted. Now he was all flying legs and arms. He rushed upon Jake and sank his teeth into his leg. The boxes clattered down. Zizzy pounced next. Timothy swept him aside as though he were chaff.

He grabbed the boxes and ran with them as he had never thought he could run. When he reached the front walk of the Dousman house he slowed down until his hard breathing became easier. Then he went up the front steps, crossed the glassed-in veranda, and lifted the knocker.

The boxes were soiled. A slow trickle of blood was dripping from a cut on one of Timothy's cheeks.

Well, I got here, Timothy thought. And I'm delivering the packages. That's all that is important now.

CHAPTER 4.

The Dousman House

◆◆◆◆◆◆◆◆◆◆◆◆◆◆◆◆◆

AN OLD FRENCH SERVANT in satin livery came to the door. He did not seem greatly shocked at Timothy's appearance. Young gentlemen who had the temerity to knock at front doors, no matter how they looked, were young gentlemen. There had been many strange guests at the Dousman house, from a Russian prince and an Indian chief to traders or voyageurs.

"Step right in, sir," said the butler and opened the heavy door, standing aside with great courtesy.

Timothy blinked in the mellow light. He found himself in a great hall from which rose stairs—not boxed-in stairs like those in the Dustin house, but curving stairs with lustrous mahogany banisters.

"Can I be of service, young man?" the old butler inquired. "Are you expected?"

"I guess so," Timothy answered. "I'm Timothy Dustin of the *Johnny Smoker*, and I'm to deliver these two packages."

"I think Mr. Derosia is in the library," the butler said. "Just follow me, please."

Timothy turned his gaze to the left, and saw the great drawing room through an archway—polished furniture upholstered in blue velvet, a graceful chandelier of priceless design, the creamy wallpaper with its gray garlands and roses.

Suddenly he was aware of something incongruous. Here he was, amid all this elegance, a disheveled urchin in soiled blue jeans, rough woolen jacket, with a smutty, bloody face, standing with his boots in the deep pile carpet. How the family would shout with merriment at home when he told them! But probably Isabel and his mother would be quite provoked.

Now the butler was propelling him into what he called the library. An older man sat reading in front of a birch fire. Timothy's eyes were on the floor in embarrassment. But the absorbed gentleman in the chair was totally unaware of his visitor's appearance.

"As soon as I've finished this chapter," he said. "Sit down. Sit down a minute."

"Yes, sir," said Timothy in a meek voice, grateful for the delay.

He sat down carefully on a rosewood chair tufted in rich red satin. He was afraid of soiling that immaculately perfect satin. He placed the boxes on the floor beside him.

The servant coughed significantly.

"What's wanted, Louis?" asked the man with the book.

"If you please, sir," the butler said, "this young gentleman to see you is from the *Johnny Smoker.*"

"The *Johnny Smoker?* Captain Dustin's boat? Why didn't you say so in the first place?" the man demanded.

He jumped to his feet, casting the book aside. He barely glanced at Timothy but noted the two packages.

"You brought them both, safely," he assured himself. "Captain Dustin gave them to you to deliver?" His tone was sharp.

"Yes, sir," Timothy answered.

"Call Emily, Louis," the man said. "Her mother also." To Timothy he confided, "The ladies will want the thrill of opening the boxes."

Emily must have been waiting, for almost at once a girl in shimmering blue satin swept into the room. She was as much of a surprise as the house had been. Her head was topped with golden curls bound with a blue ribbon, and her eyes were as blue as aquamarines.

"They came?" she asked, breathless with anticipation of delight.

"Yes," the man assured her. "The Captain's dependable, you know. I rather expected him to deliver the goods in person, but he sent a messenger."

He turned toward Timothy and for the first time took in his unkempt appearance, appraising him from his tousled hair to his unpolished boots.

"Well, well!" He lifted shaggy brows, much amused. "And who are you, my lad?"

"Timothy Dustin," the inappropriate guest answered. "I'm Captain Dustin's son, though I assure you, sir, he'd be mightily ashamed of the way I look. He did tell me to wash, sir, but I got only as far as my hands."

"Look at his hands!" The girl shrieked with laughter.

"I had a little trouble after I washed them," Timothy admitted.

"Why, you're hurt!" The girl's tone softened amazingly. "Isn't that blood?"

Timothy set the boxes down hastily and began to rub the bloodstained corner of one of them. "I do hope it won't spoil what's inside—whatever *is* inside."

"We'll see what's inside," the man declared, and turned, as a tall, handsome woman in black silk entered the room. Timothy had never before seen so much jet or so many ruffles on a black frock. Behind her came a dashing young man, equally elegant.

"Henri!" Timothy shouted in amazement.

His embarrassment disappeared and his flashing

smile shone through the blood and grime on his face. Henri stood, hesitant, for just a split second. Then he rushed across the room and grasped Timothy's hand, slapping him on the shoulder.

"Dustin!" he shouted. "Timothy Dustin! You were so busy I didn't bother you on the boat. You've met my father, I see. This is Emily, my sister, and this is my mother. Father, Timothy's the expert shot I told you about, the fellow that Queenie robbed of the ducks because she was so ashamed of me."

The two ladies gently offered to cleanse Timothy's cut, but he said, "There's nothing the matter with me that a face washing won't cure."

"Come along then," Henri cried. "Wash up and let the family see what you look like."

"Just a moment." Henri's father held up his hand. "Suppose we open these boxes first. After all, they are heavily insured, and Timothy here would like to carry back a receipt that shows the goods have arrived in fine condition. Anything could have happened to the boxes in transit. Other boxes could have been substituted for them. They were not out of your hands, Timothy?"

Timothy thought quickly.

"No, sir," he answered. "I did set them on a hedge to hit a fellow. But I didn't give him time to exchange them."

Mr. Derosia was opening the packages with a

hand that shook. Emily ran to a desk and brought out some long shears with which she snipped ribbons, while her father broke seals of wax, heavily stamped, saying, "These look like the proper seals."

"I'm sure they are, sir," Timothy decided. "But isn't it strange that my father never made much of the value to me?"

"Not at all," Mr. Derosia answered. "If too much fuss had been made, the shipment would have attracted attention. What did the boy look like that you stopped to hit?"

"Tall and dark," Timothy answered. "Somebody at the landing called him Jake. There was a smaller boy, too, named Zizzy."

"The Flint boys," Mr. Derosia said. "They're a bad lot, both of them."

"Flint?" Timothy inquired. "There's a Flint boy who lives in Reads Landing. Name is Ash Flint."

But the Derosias were paying no attention to Timothy now. They stood breathless with expectancy.

Mr. Derosia lifted the cover from the larger box and swept aside the swirl of tissue paper in which a garment had been wrapped. He lifted up a cape of white fur with some dots of black, and Timothy saw that it was an ermine cape and that the dots were the tips of ermine tails. A fabulous thing! The most exquisite thing he had ever seen in furs! Soft. Rich. White.

Expectancy hung in the air as the second box was opened. This time the fur was dark—a sable scarf with a sheen that was far more beautiful than the fur on any live sable.

Mr. Derosia, delighted that his purchases had come through safely, signed a receipt and handed it to Timothy.

"We're guests at the Dousman house," he said, "for some time. If the *Johnny Smoker* makes another trip, stop in. And watch out for the Flints."

CHAPTER 5.

Haunts!

BACK IN READS LANDING once more, Timothy wondered if he had dreamed his visit to the Dousman house and his delivering of the fabulous gifts. But he could not quite forget the Flints and their attack on him.

He was reminded of them again when Ash Flint, who worked at Murgner's tannery, appeared the very first morning after his return. Timothy found him standing beside Billy in the back yard while Billy finished his work on the muskrat skins he had accumulated.

"Got any relatives by the name of Flint in Prairie du Chien?" Timothy inquired abruptly.

"Yes," Ash answered. "I've got cousins."

"Do you hear from them?" Timothy inquired.

"Once in a while," the boy answered. "They come to visit sometimes."

"Well, I don't think much of them," Timothy stated abruptly.

To make up for Timothy's rudeness Billy said, "Come on, Ash; look at my peltries. I've got over sixty muskrat pelts in the woodshed. Has Mr. Murgner many furs this year?"

"No," Ash answered. "He's handling mostly beef, veal, and sheep hides—tans 'em and sells 'em to the factories for shoes, you know. We'll ship our last packs by the *Johnny Smoker* to St. Louis, if your father's going to make another trip. It's pretty late though."

"Not for Father," Billy boasted. "The *Johnny Smoker* will come in on her last voyage of the season through surface ice. You'll see."

"Captain Dustin's a wonder," Ash declared, and Timothy felt ashamed of his resentment. Surely Ash was not responsible for what his cousins did.

The *Johnny Smoker* was to pull out the next day on her last trip of the season to St. Louis. When Timothy went into the house, he found his father and mother sitting in front of the sitting room stove with its cheery oak fire, discussing plans for the winter. Cold wind blew about the house in leafy gusts.

"See if you can get a nice hindquarter of beef, William," Mrs. Dustin suggested, busily hemming a ruffle of red wool plaid by hand.

"I went into Burkhardt's Market yesterday," the Captain told his wife, "and Rudy was quite provoked that I wouldn't take a front quarter."

"Rudy knows I want steaks," Mrs. Dustin said,

impatiently. "Does he think I can serve sausage or stew to the minister?"

"Speaking of ministers," Captain Dustin drawled, "I think I just saw the parson pass the window."

Immediately there was a knock at the front door and the Captain admitted the Reverend Soule. "I was passing the old Ferguson house," he said, "when I noticed these medicinal plants among the weeds, and I knew you dried them for neighbors. So I brought you a bunch of them."

Mrs. Dustin exclaimed over the thick leaves of fennel, the red tassels of the smartweed, and the bushy catnip intended for Africa, the cat.

"The old Ferguson house looks neglected, standing empty like that," the minister said as he took the rocker. "I didn't know the family, but I've heard they were fine people. That was a terrible tragedy, the parents' being killed. Why doesn't the son, Gerald, and his family live in the old home instead of that cabin on Sanborn's Point?"

"Takes time to get over memories," Captain Dustin pointed out.

"I wish the place could see some young life," the minister pursued. "The house is handsome."

"But it's haunted!" said the Captain in a hollow voice.

"So I've heard," said the minister with a twinkle in his eye. Then he added, "I saw Gerald Ferguson in town today. He said he would be up to see you."

The Captain tipped back his chair for a better view out of the window. He saw Gerald Ferguson, climbing the hill road in his rickety wagon, pulled by his old brown mare.

Timothy, running down from the woodlot where he had been helping Billy and Johnny Sterling, took Gerald's horse. Mrs. Dustin hastened to the back door. The others in the sitting room could hear Gerald's voice.

"My wife sent you folks a couple of roasted mallards," the pleasant voice said, "stuffed with wild rice. Mary knows how much you like wild rice, Mrs. Dustin."

The pastor soon rose to go, and then Billy and Johnny Sterling came back from the woodlot and Rella and Mary bounced in from school. The whole family and Gerald Ferguson sat down to dinner.

It was an unwritten rule that the Ferguson tragedy must never be mentioned to Gerald. Today everyone was amazed when the Captain, in front of them all, broached the subject.

"The parson," Captain Dustin informed Gerald, "wanted me to ask you why you don't move back to the old home? Guess he wants Mary for a Sunday School teacher, and he probably wants to add your two youngsters to the Sunday School roll."

"I guess I haven't the courage," Gerald said

quietly. "It would remind me too much of what happened to the family. I wish I had the courage of my father. He was a free trader, you know. Maybe he made his mistake, not working in with the American Fur Company. As it was, he didn't have protection. But he did a big business. Often he spent several seasons in the woods before he brought down his furs."

He paused, and the Dustins knew what was coming. Because the Sioux were not on the warpath at the time, Gerald's father had taken his family with him on that last trip. But he had not reckoned with the powerful fur-stealing trader who had hired a party of embittered Indians to work for him.

"I can still see that last cargo," Gerald said. "There were twenty-four bales of fur. My father had waited until the fur was thick to buy his pelts—mink in its prime, wild silver fox, marten soft as silk, muskrat, fisher, and otter. It was something to see. I was a small boy but I still remember it. We were to turn over the twenty-four bales to Colonel Dousman at Prairie du Chien and, on the last evening of our voyage, we camped just below Wabasha."

The Dustins could imagine the scene—the birch-bark caravan with colorful painting on the bows, the camp fires, and the busy helpers preparing the evening meal.

"The trader and the Sioux he had hired were

camped up in the hills. They came down on us and massacred the entire party—my father, his friends and guides, even my mother. You all know the story. They made off with the furs."

"All twenty-four bales?" Timothy asked.

"Yes, all of them."

"How did you escape?"

"I was wandering in the woods, picking wild strawberries, and they didn't find me."

"What happened to you?" Rella cried.

"Indian Joe found me and took me to the Chippewa camp," Gerald continued. "The Chippewas had seen the attack but came too late to save my people. They pursued the party of Sioux but somehow the trader managed to hide the furs."

"Then the furs are *somewhere*," Timothy put in. "They were never put on the market?"

"Never," Gerald answered. "They were too valuable not to be traced."

"But what happened to you then?" Rella inquired.

"I lived with the Chippewas for a long time. I learned to like them. They were very kind to me."

"That must all be ten years ago," Mrs. Dustin figured.

"Twelve, Mrs. Dustin," Gerald said. "I was ten when Indian Joe took me. I'm twenty-two now, going on twenty-three."

"This is the first time, Gerald, that you've talked

of this to us," the Captain put in. "I am glad that you can. It means that you have come through your trials with a fine courage."

"Not quite," Gerald said wistfully. "But at least I am going into the house again. Mary wants me to get a couple of old coats from a chest in the attic. She's going to make coats for the children. People say the house is haunted."

"You know better than that," Mrs. Dustin said briskly.

"Yes, of course," Gerald replied quite as briskly, then his voice trailed off. "They say you can hear strains of my mother's harp and that sometimes my father clumps across the attic floor in his boots—and there are no footprints."

A little shiver went around the table.

Timothy got to his feet.

"Maybe I can help you, Gerald," he offered. "I'm not afraid of haunts. I'll go with you."

When they reached the deserted old house, Gerald tied the horse to the hitching post, and then he and Timothy waded through the deep grass and weeds around to the back door. They entered the kitchen and walked silently through the dining room with its cupboards of fine dishes. The crystals on the hanging lamp above the mahogany table still sparkled in the early afternoon sun that filtered in through the curtains. A film of dust covered everything.

Gerald did not pause, and Timothy followed him up the stairs to the second floor, glancing briefly into the bedrooms, whose mirrors were clouded from the cold of many winters. Then up the narrow steps to the attic!

They stood for a long moment, trying to accustom themselves to the dim light from the one window at the far end. Then Gerald lifted the top of the chest near the door and handed Timothy the two coats Mary had asked him to get.

Suddenly Gerald grasped Timothy's arm tightly. "Did you hear that?" he whispered.

"Hear what?" Timothy whispered back, and his knees felt weak.

Then they both heard it. From somewhere below them in the silent house came a sound—a distinct thump. The two ran down the attic stairs and had reached the dining room before either spoke. As they stood there uncertainly, they heard footsteps below them—in the basement.

Gerald rushed to the trap door in the pantry off the kitchen and drew it up.

"Who's there?" Gerald demanded, and Timothy shouted after, "Who's there?"

"Jake Flint," a voice answered. "Zizzy is with me. We saw the horse and wagon outside and thought maybe we could help. The kitchen door was locked, so we crawled in through a basement window."

Jake came up the basement steps as he spoke. Behind him appeared his younger brother.

"How long have you been in this house?" Gerald demanded.

"We just came," Jake answered.

"Well, you had no business here," Gerald said sharply. "Don't come trespassing again."

The two Flint boys hastily departed and Timothy turned to Gerald. "I don't like those two coming here," he said. "They're not to be trusted. They tried to steal some packages that I was delivering to the Dousman house down at Prairie du Chien. We'd better see what they were up to in the basement."

"There isn't a thing down there they could steal," Gerald said. "They were probably just snooping around. They won't come back now that we've given them a scare."

CHAPTER 6.

Johnny Smoker Gifts

❖❖❖❖❖❖❖❖❖❖❖❖❖❖❖

THE ST. LOUIS TRIP of the *Johnny Smoker* was to be the next-to-the-last trip of the season. The ponds were already frozen over, and the only leaves that remained on the trees were those on the brown burr-oak. The hills were brown now except on frosty mornings when hoarfrost blossoms hung in the occasional pine or cedar that grew among the hardwoods. Rivers were mushy, with shore ice crackling, but the channel of the Mississippi remained open, a blue-black ribbon that defied weather.

Water pails on benches froze to the bottom and were no longer of use. Housewives complained because of the mess when the men had to wash up in the kitchens.

Timothy was lonely for Billy and Johnny Sterling, for they had departed with the Captain. Timothy could not afford to miss school, the Captain had decided.

The saucy little chipmunks had betaken themselves underground. Muskrats sat on top of their huge houses, and the men gathered around the stove in Duerre's store predicted, as usual, that it would be a long, cold winter. They could tell, they maintained, by the size of the muskrat houses.

Some of the folks who might be shut in when the snow was deep began to make their fall visits. Mamie Rand, who lived by herself on the edge of town and therefore had no "menfolk to do her chores," called at the Dustin house one Saturday morning. Mrs. Dustin was busy with her week's baking, but she made Mamie a pot of tea to tide her over until dinner time.

Mamie drew the younger children to her by the fascination of her tales. Mrs. Dustin pooh-poohed them, but Timothy enjoyed Mamie's woodlore, which was often fantastic—and sometimes amazingly accurate. On this particular morning, Rella and Mary crowded together on one chair, across from their busy mother, to listen to Mamie, and Timothy stood behind his little sisters, absorbed.

From her pocket, which was somewhere in the voluminous folds of her skirt, Mamie extracted a frozen caterpillar.

"Don't put that thing on my bread board!" Mrs. Dustin begged.

Mamie did not take offense at Mrs. Dustin's tone, and Rella said, "Here! Put him down on my handkerchief."

"A handkerchief is worse," Mrs. Dustin scolded.

"I'll hold him on my lap," Mamie offered. "I just wanted to show you children something. You can't learn everything in school. Now look at this here caterpillar: he can tell you a lot. You see the three parts of the caterpillar's color, black at both ends and brown in the middle. Well, the part near the head is the fall, the middle is the winter, and the end is the spring. I never knew a caterpillar to lie about the length of the seasons or the kind. See! We had an early, cold fall and short. Now isn't that so? Notice the dark brown middle: that means a long, cold winter. If the brown was light in color, it would mean a mild winter. Then look at the short, dark tail. That means a short spring and quick-like, because the color changes sudden. A short, early spring, turning sudden."

"That's the way it usually is," Mrs. Dustin said complacently. "I've known freezes in May and then it turned so hot on the last day of May that the children took off their winter underwear to go barefooted."

"If you'd 'a' noticed the caterpillars that year," Mamie Rand said, "you'd have known the weather was coming on sudden like that. I say that folks that's too persnickery to pay attention to what the woods creatures tells them have to take what comes."

No one minded Mamie's peppery tone, Mrs. Dustin least of all.

"The Captain'll make this trip and maybe another," Mamie prophesied.

"I wouldn't doubt that," said Mrs. Dustin.

"Bring home a lot of presents, I suppose," Mamie mused. "He's one man thinks of the folks at home."

"I wish he'd think of himself," Mrs. Dustin worried. "He needs an overcoat."

Mamie stayed for dinner and she stayed for supper. Whenever she visited, she always stayed for both meals. Not that she made herself a nuisance; her calls were widely spaced. There were enough friends to "go around," as she herself expressed it.

Timothy, carrying a basket of baking—a loaf of bread, a wedge of jelly layer cake, some biscuits, and half a mince pie—politely saw Mamie home. She always went home by daylight, and her hostesses saw to it that supper was served early. Only owls, Mamie often remarked, stayed out at night, and she wasn't quite wise enough for that. Wiping the dishes for Isabel after supper, she declared, "Well, it's time that decent folks were abed and rogues were on their way."

She always said the same thing, and Rella and Mary could fairly see the rogues scuttling.

Ducks and geese flying south made patterns in the sky above Timothy as he hurried home, his coat held tight about him. The last flights surely, for hard, tiny particles of snow were filling the air! As he hurried over the frosty ground, he heard, first with his mind, then with his heart, the familiar, mellow whistle of a boat. His discomfort vanished like snow before a Chinook wind, and he raced for the levee. He was not surprised to see Mary and Rella come running down the hill in their pussy hoods of Angora yarn, red ribbons tied under their chins and red mittens on their hands. Their capes billowed out behind them.

"The *Johnny Smoker!*" Mary and Rella were shouting. "The *Johnny Smoker!*"

As though the words were a magic incantation, doors opened along the streets, and out of houses and stores, hotels and taverns, men, women, and children came running. It was not unusual for the town to meet boats, but a boat this late in the season was an event.

The roustabout who jumped off the bow with the landing rope ran through crackling shore ice. With much jesting Captain Dustin came down the gangplank. "A little ice isn't going to stop the *Johnny Smoker*," he shouted.

Evidently someone else in the crowd had the same idea, for the hardware man, Joe James, called out, "How about gettin' me some hardware from St. Paul, Cap'n Bill?"

"Sure," Captain Dustin responded. "Want me to bring it, double or nothing?"

"Not on your life," Joe James shouted. "No more betting against the *Johnny Smoker*."

"Hello, youngsters," Johnny Sterling said in his mild voice. "Brought you something different this time. A surprise."

"And I brought you a treat too. A surprise," Billy declared, lifting a box to his shoulders.

"Let me take that lumpy gunny sack," Timothy offered, and Johnny Sterling boosted it to the willing shoulders.

In the Dustin kitchen Johnny Sterling proudly produced from the gunny sack a whole bunch of bananas, something the little girls had never seen before.

"They've ripened just enough," Johnny decided. "I like them best when there are little dark specks in the yellow. Here, Rella, here's a perfect one! Here, Mary, a beauty for you! Help yourselves, everybody."

Everybody watched as he pulled back the peel of a large, perfect banana and took a good bite. The others did the same, but Mary ran to the back door and spat hers out.

"I don't like it!" She took a long drink of water from the tin dipper on the kitchen washstand.

Mrs. Dustin laid her own slightly tasted fruit on

the table, saying, "I guess one has to get used to them."

Isabel added, "I'm sure they're delicious once you do."

Timothy was more frank.

"If that's the kind of food Southerners have to eat, me for the North! What's in the box?"

"Persimmons!" Billy announced. "Recommended by Johnny Sterling."

Johnny looked hopeful. But the persimmons fared even worse than the bananas.

"Well, Johnny," Captain Dustin sympathized, "it's just too bad you made that hole in your wages."

"Father, you should reimburse him," Mrs. Dustin decided.

"Who—me?" The Captain gave his wife a comical look. "*You* were the one who looked the gift horse in the mouth, you and the children."

His wife changed the subject. "William," she said, "did you get that coat?"

"I don't need an overcoat," Captain Dustin insisted.

"I thought we'd hashed that over, William," Mrs. Dustin persisted. "You're not as young as you once were, and Mamie Rand says it's going to be a long, cold winter."

Laughing, the Captain said, "I was only teasing.

Richards Gordon is making me an overcoat—up in St. Paul."

"And how are you going to get to St. Paul, Captain Bill?" Mrs. Dustin inquired. "Put a giant bobsled under your side-wheeler?"

At the picture their mother's words evoked, Mary and Rella laughed outright, almost forgetting their disappointment over the gifts from the South. Their father, delving into one of his big pockets, tossed one striped bag on the table, then another. The two little girls fairly pounced upon them.

"Candy," the Captain informed Johnny Sterling, with a spacious grin, "speaks a universal language."

Mrs. Dustin faced the Captain with spirit.

"Shall we get back to the matter of the overcoat, William?" she asked. "How are you going to get that overcoat in St. Paul?"

"Going after it with the *Johnny Smoker*," Captain Dustin boasted. "Lake Pepin is still open—will be until the first of December. Maybe have to get out and cut a path in some parts of the river, but we'll get through."

Mrs. Dustin sighed, but mostly with admiration.

"Since you bought the *Johnny Smoker*," she said, "there isn't anything you won't tackle."

"How about taking me along, Father?" Timothy inquired, as he lounged in the doorway between the sitting room and kitchen. "I could stoke to St. Paul the same as I did to Prairie du Chien."

"Not a bad idea," the Captain decided. "Give Billy and Johnny a chance to get a good supply of muskrat skins. They're running good this season."

Luckily for the Captain, a spell of open weather followed his announcement, and the trip to St. Paul was made without incident.

Timothy, for the first time in his life, visited the wholesale district of the capital with his father and gazed with awe at the vast storerooms filled with fur packs. He met the dignified Mr. Richards Gordon of whom he had heard so much.

Mr. Gordon's firm, it seemed, was up against a problem. Mink, so popular in Europe a few years before, had gone out of style. The great numbers of mink peltries accumulated by the partners were unsalable in Europe. Something had to be done.

When Captain Dustin came to leave the warehouse a few days later, he carried with him a large box.

The weather was, as the Captain put it, "catching cold," and the trip back through Lake Pepin was stormy and miserable. The little side-wheeler churned up slush and fought buffeting blocks of ice. It ground surface ice as it neared the shore. Timothy was more weary than he had been after the trip to Prairie du Chien, but more elated.

Mrs. Dustin had a good hot supper waiting, and the Captain was soon sitting in the rocking chair in the sitting room, replete with food and drink—and satisfaction.

"Well, Permelia," he said, "the season's over. You'll have me under foot for a few months, pottering around and getting in your way."

"That will be wonderful, William," Mrs. Dustin said, her eyes shining. "And now let's see your overcoat. I hope you didn't scrimp on it. I hope you got yourself a good warm buffalo garment."

"I did better than that," the Captain boasted, though with some misgiving.

He undid the rope that held the box he had laid on the floor back of the stove, and lifted out a great garment. He put it on, and Mrs. Dustin gasped as she saw her husband in a mink coat, the fur on the outside.

"Wherever did you get that?" she gasped. "And why?"

"It's the style in St. Paul," said Captain Dustin. "No sale for mink in Europe, so Richards Gordon is giving us menfolk the benefit of the surplus peltries. Mink for the price of buffalo."

"You'll never wear that in Reads Landing," Mrs. Dustin prophesied. "The town would follow you about."

"So you don't want your husband to set the style, Permelia?"

"It isn't that, William. It's just that I know you'll never wear it." Mrs. Dustin sighed.

"Maybe you're right at that," the Captain acknowledged. "If I don't, maybe you can make it up into muffs for you and the girls."

CHAPTER 7.

A Mirage on a Beaver Hunt

◆◆◆◆◆◆◆◆◆◆◆◆◆◆◆◆

TIMOTHY HAD NOT SEEN Henri Derosia since the trip of the *Johnny Smoker* to Prairie du Chien and his visit to the Dousman house. When Henri appeared suddenly at the front door of the Dustin home on an evening so cold that footsteps squeaked in the snow, Timothy's shout of welcome brought Billy to the door too. The two boys dragged the guest in to the stove with its cheerful fire crackling behind the red isinglass.

Mrs. Dustin brought in some red apples, while Isabel, Rella, and Mary proffered bowls of corn. Then they rushed back into the kitchen where the sound of popping continued, as the covered frying pan scraped back and forth across the hot stove lids. The Captain, seated at his desk, where he was checking fur prices, reached out his hand.

"Well, young man," he inquired, "what are you doing in Reads Landing? Expect me to get the *Johnny Smoker* out and give you a lift back to Prairie du Chien again?"

"Hardly, sir," Henri answered, "though I wouldn't

be much surprised at anything the *Johnny Smoker* could do. My folks are going into the fur business. Father wants me to learn about trapping. He thinks there's going to be a big sale for beaver because of the demand in Europe for beaver hats. I've been hoping to go on a beaver hunt with Timothy."

"Billy's the beaver expert," Timothy offered.

"Maybe I could go with Billy then—if he'd bother with me," Henri said wistfully, remembering his hunting experience with Timothy. "I came up on the stage and am going back day after tomorrow. By the way, the two Flint boys were on the stage, coming to visit their cousin. Could we make a trip tomorrow? I'd have all day."

"Tomorrow it is," Billy agreed. "You and Timothy and I will go. Johnny Sterling's helping some of the neighbors cut wood."

"We mustn't take all the beavers in one colony," said Henri with boyish candor. "Father says to be sure to leave one pair for each dam."

He wondered why all the Dustins laughed, until Billy said, "The beavers themselves will see to that."

"So Father was teasing me," Henri decided good-naturedly. "I wonder if he meant it when he said I mustn't do too much damage to any one dam."

"He did mean that," Billy said, soberly. "If you do a little damage to a dam, the beavers will swim up to make repairs. That's the best and easiest way to get them—just whack them on the heads with a stout stick and take home a reasonable catch. Losing a few beavers never yet discouraged a colony. They'll keep on living in the same place and raise more beavers. You can always depend then on that location. But if you destroy the dam completely, your beavers will move. And they'll never come back. See?"

Henri understood. He felt warm and comfortable, not only in body but in spirit. He was enjoying the hospitality of the Dustin house.

Isabel, coming in from the kitchen, persuaded the boys to go to bed early and promised them a hearty breakfast and a packet of food. The Captain wished them good luck, and Mrs. Dustin added her good wishes.

"I see Lapham and Company has listed muskrat at twelve cents," the Captain remarked. "Large, prime beavers bring two-fifty."

"That's the kind we'll catch," Timothy boasted. "Eh, Henri?"

"Large, prime beavers," Henri agreed.

Henri said he had never before eaten such a big breakfast—buckwheat cakes with butter and maple syrup, sausages, coffee, and apple sauce. There were doughnuts and cookies to fill in any empty cracks in the hunter's appetite. Henri was thrilled with the clothes that the Dustins provided for him—wool underwear of red flannel and the heavy, soft socks that Isabel and Mrs. Dustin had knitted; the moccasins made by Indians; and the deerskin trousers and the fine white doeskin jackets that the boys belted in with bright woolen scarves. On their heads they wore beaver caps pulled down over their ears, the rough fur sticking out in all directions.

"You know beaver has to be scraped to remove the long hairs," Billy explained when Henri said that his father's beaver cap wasn't anything like this. "These caps haven't been tanned, just dried."

It was still dark when the three boys left the house. As they started across the river at the levee, Billy sounded the ice with a stout stick for air holes. The sky was getting lighter in the east; and, just as the tardy winter sun peeped over the horizon, Billy gave an excited cry.

"Look!" He had turned towards Lake Pepin. On its great expanse of glittering, mirror-like ice stood a city. It had not been there a few moments before. Yet the town had been transported, by some magic, from the shore to the lake, a city of resplendent beauty with opalescent hues and rainbow mists wavering through its fairylike streets. As the rays of the fast-rising sun dispelled the mist, the city slowly faded from their sight.

"Indian Joe says," Billy remarked, "that a mirage means a storm."

"No storm today," Timothy decided. "It's too dry and bright as the sun gets up. See how the ice glitters! We'll have fine weather today to teach Henri about beavers. Henri, what do you know about beavers except that the Indians like beaver-tail soup?"

"I didn't know that," Henri admitted. "All I know is that beavers plaster mud on their lodges with their tails."

Both Timothy and Billy shouted, "You're wrong!"

"Well, tell me," Henri begged. "I'm willing to learn."

"All right," Billy agreed. "We'll begin with the beaver's tail. The beaver uses his tail as a rudder when he's swimming on the surface. He submerges! Now he uses his tail to keep him at the depth he wants to be. He comes up to cut a tree. What better brace could he have than that big, fat tail? We come along, and he suspects that we've come for no good. With his tail, he slaps the top of the water to warn his kits."

"Kits?" Henri inquired.

"Yes. Their young are kits," Billy said. "Did you ever see a beaver cut a tree?"

"Yes," Henri answered. "He gnaws through the trunk."

"Not exactly." Timothy took Henri's arm and steered him towards the Wisconsin bank where a young tree stood apart from the others. "He cuts like a woodsman. Watch me. I'm a beaver. I cut a notch above and a notch below. Then I pry out the wood between, making plenty of chips."

"If the beaver cut right through the tree," Billy added, "it might fall on him. So he leaves an inch or more so that the tree will crack down more slowly and give him a chance to scamper out of the way."

"I once saw a baby beaver," Henri said, "with front paws that looked just like little hands."

"They use the paws like hands," Billy said. "You must have seen beavers carrying mud and stones and grasses hugged against their chins. All the plastering and smoothing you thought they did with their tails, they actually do with their paws."

The three boys climbed up through some partly submerged willows and hazel brush. They went single file through woods with bare trees and firs heavy-laden with snow. They came eventually to a large sheet of ice, dotted here and there by sticks. There seemed to be piles of brush at one end, where a miniature lake stood. The lake was frozen over and there was no sign of life. But Billy said, "Here's one of the beaver colonies."

"Where are the beavers?" Henri inquired. "Do they hibernate all winter, like bears? I've seen some that were fat enough."

"No," said Timothy dryly, "you'll see."

Billy had begun to hack two big holes in the brushwork. It was just below what Timothy called the spillway. The sounds of his ax crackled in the still air.

He paused for a few moments. "Beavers work as hard, if not harder, in the winter than they do in the summer," he said. "They make tunnels to connect with the bank holes. They scoop out runways in the upper part of the dam, and they improve the floor of the colony towards spring so there will be a thick carpet of fine shavings for the kits when they arrive."

"Water's coming through!" Henri shouted all of a sudden.

At first the green-blue water only seeped up; then it began to rush forth. It poured out over the hard ice, and Henri began to realize why they had smeared so much tallow on their boots for waterproofing.

Billy and Timothy now stood on either side of the breakage, clubs in their hands. There was not a sound in the cold air but the rapid breathing of the boys. Then as though an alarm had sounded, beavers began to rise to the surface.

"Repair crew!" Henri rejoiced.

Billy knocked out three industrious animals and Timothy got two. Henri made no attempt. It was not until he had visited his third dam that he captured one of the biggest and most beautiful beavers he had ever seen.

"Your father will be proud of you," Timothy decided.

"Large and prime," Henri boasted. "*Your* father will be proud of me too."

A light wind sprang up suddenly, carrying with it tiny particles of snow. Without a word the boys rushed the work of skinning their game. That mirage had meant something.

"We've all we can carry," Billy decided. "We won't wait even long enough to make tea. Isabel wrapped up sandwiches for us with plenty of meat in them. Here's one for each of us. We'll eat as we walk."

The snow glistened at first in the sunlight, then shone pale gold as through a curtain. It was not long before the curtain had grown so heavy that the boys could not see through it at all. Henri was worried, but Timothy said, "Trust Billy. He knows his way like a compass."

"I think I can find the track we made coming

over," said Billy, "but we must be roped together and walk slowly. I'll sound the ice all the way."

He tied a rope about his own waist, took his pack in one hand and his stout stick in the other. Henri seized the rope and followed close behind. Timothy, tying a knot in the end of the rope lest he drop it, brought up the rear.

Henri insisted they were going in the wrong direction, but when Billy said, "If you are so sure of the way, maybe you'd like to take the stick," Henri grew quiet.

"It does seem as if we'd never get there," Timothy complained.

"We have to play safe in this storm," Billy said. Even as he spoke, he stumbled over a boardwalk.

Now the three knew their way by heart. With Henri between them, the Dustin boys reached the house, deposited their peltries in the summer kitchen, and pulled off their red mittens to warm their hands in front of the kitchen range.

No supper had ever tasted so good to Henri as the cold meat, fried potatoes, and hot stewed tomatoes. No cookies were ever so good as the fat molasses cookies. Nor had any other apple sauce the flavor of the sauce Isabel spooned into huge glass dishes.

Mr. Dustin examined the peltries, pronounced them fine, and gave Henri the message from the

Union House that he was to be ready to take the morning stage.

◇◇◇◇◇◇◇
◇◇◇◇◇◇◇

It was not until Henri had disappeared down the hill the following morning that Billy said, "Guess I'll add the beaver hides to the muskrat peltries in the woodshed. Henri took only that big fellow of his to show his father."

"I'll help you," Timothy offered.

At the woodshed door Billy pulled out the peg that latched it. He undid the catch, pushed in the door, and looked about, mystified. The woodshed was empty of peltries. Not one muskrat remained on the walls. Shingles and all had disappeared.

"They've been stolen," Billy exclaimed.

"Stolen," Timothy echoed.

CHAPTER 8.

On the Trail of the Muskrat Peltries

◆◆◆◆◆◆◆◆◆◆◆◆◆◆◆◆

TIMOTHY AND BILLY had the same thought at the same time. There was only one way that the furs could be spirited out of Reads Landing without detection and that was by stage.

"I saw the stage pull out just a minute ago while I was pumping a pail of water for Isabel," Billy remembered. "The four horses turned past the haunted house. I could see a couple of boys inside and some fellow in a buffalo coat."

"The Flints!" Timothy yelled. "Henri said they came on the stage with him the other day. I had trouble with them at Prairie du Chien, and a while back Gerald and I found them snooping around in the basement of the Ferguson house. They're a pair of thieves."

"Go after them," Billy advised, "but keep calm."

Rella came running out, and Billy hastily explained what had happened.

"I saw some sled tracks outside the fence near the birch tree," Rella said. "Great wide tracks!"

The boys paid no attention to her.

"Sled tracks," Billy said. "Sled tracks are everywhere."

Timothy raced down the hill towards the stage, still plainly in sight on the river road that ran along the base of the snow-clad hills. The stage was making good time. The horses seemed to know that they were on the last lap of their journey. It was only three miles to Wabasha where a warm barn and a measure of oats awaited them. The stage would go on from there with fresh horses.

Timothy's shout followed the stage, but to no avail. He thought he saw someone wave as if in answer to his wildly gesticulating arms, but the driver did not slow up.

He ran after the stagecoach until he could run no more. He dropped down on a snow bank, his breath labored, his lungs on fire. His heart thudded against his ribs. He was opposite the Murgner barn. A horse looked curiously at him over the half door that Ash opened on mild winter days to let in fresh air. Someone was working inside, forking fresh straw to make a clean bed.

"That you, Ash Flint?" Fresh signs of vigor replaced Timothy's exhaustion.

"Yep," said Ash.

"Those cousins of yours stole our furs and are running away with them on the stagecoach."

"What do you mean?"

"The furs are gone and I know those two are dishonest. They must have stolen the furs."

"You're wrong, Timothy." Ash came out of the barn door, blinking in the crystal white world that glittered all about the shabby tannery. "I saw them off on the stage myself, and all they had were their carpet bags and an old portmanteau full of butternuts that Mrs. Murgner gave them."

"I'll bet that portmanteau isn't full of butternuts now. I'll bet it's full of furs. How you have anything to do with those scamps . . ."

"All right," said Ash. "If you think they took the furs, why don't you have the stagecoach searched?"

"I tried to catch it. Didn't you see me? This is a fine time to talk."

"Don't stop to talk then. You take Prince and ride after the stage. You're sure to catch it, because the driver changes horses at Wabasha." Ash was putting the bit into Prince's mouth as he spoke, and then he proffered his hand to help Timothy mount. "Bareback is faster than if I took time to put on a saddle. Get going."

He slapped Prince's rump and Prince ambled out of the yard.

The rumbling stage had reached the frozen swamp at the edge of Wabasha and had slowed because of the drifts that had blown in on the curves. Timothy managed to urge Prince past the stage and onto the low bridge that crossed a slough into the town.

He slid off the horse's back and stood, facing the oncoming stage. When he raised his arms, the double team came to a halt so sudden that the driver almost lost his balance on the high seat and passengers began to shout inquiries.

"What's wrong?" the driver yelled from his seat.

"Somebody stole our furs and took them on your stagecoach," Timothy explained. "Will you please search for them?"

"I will not!" The driver swore roundly. "Stopping my stage for a couple of squirrel pelts and a coonskin tail! Out of my way!"

He lifted his handful of reins in his heavy driving gloves. A powerful voice from the rear of the stage boomed forth with such authority that the driver's gesture remained frozen.

"You'll stop for *me*, driver." A huge man in an immense buffalo overcoat climbed down the back steps of the coach and lumbered around to the driver's seat. "You may not be willing to stop your coach and make a search for this youngster, but you'll do it for me all right. If we've got thieves on this stage or stolen goods, it's our business to find them."

He threw open his overcoat and revealed a shining silver star.

"Sheriff of Wabasha County," he announced.

"George Young's the name. Now, driver, everybody knows that nobody in Reads Landing would steal a toothpick. But things might be stolen *from* Reads. Come here, my boy."

Timothy felt a bit nervous. He had once seen the sheriff in action when several rivermen from the Chippewa had fought with the Reads Landing roustabouts, and never again did he want to witness such swift punishment. The sheriff's billy had laid the drunken men out right and left. George Young never minced matters.

For the first time since he had raced down the hill at Reads on his mission, Timothy hesitated. What if the furs shouldn't be on the stagecoach? But of course they were. Of course! He could actually see them in the old portmanteau that was supposed to hold butternuts.

"How many furs?" the sheriff inquired. "And have you any suspicion of who the thieves are?"

"Sixty prime muskrat hides," Timothy answered promptly, "and I know who the thieves are. I can even point out the exact luggage that contains the peltries."

"Fine!" the sheriff approved. "All right. Point it out!"

"The Flint boys have them in an old portmanteau," Timothy informed the sheriff. "They tried to steal from me once before in Prairie du Chien."

The sheriff ordered the two boys to get out of the stagecoach and to bring their luggage with them. They obeyed, but arrogantly. Jake gave Timothy a defiant glare, while the younger boy snickered.

"They want the portmanteau, Zizzy," Jake ordered. "Bring it out! There it is, Sheriff."

Henri came to the door of the stagecoach to inquire the cause of Timothy's trouble. He shared his friend's indignation.

The sheriff looked into the two carpet bags first —just to make a thorough job of things, he explained. The bags contained a few soiled clothes.

The portmanteau was strapless. It was held together with frayed pieces of rope and soiled string.

"Lend me your knife," the sheriff said brusquely.

Before Timothy had time to draw his own knife from his pocket, Jake had handed the sheriff his.

"Bold to the last ditch!" Henri whispered to Timothy.

The sheriff lifted the cover up all along the sides, then pulled it off. Timothy gulped, with a sudden sick rush of alarm. Over the snowy roadside tumbled a flood of butternuts. Passengers on the stagecoach began to guffaw.

But the sheriff shouted, "Pretty clever, using a layer of butternuts to cover the peltries."

He tumbled the portmanteau upside down and

lifted it from its contents. Unbelieving, he stirred his hands through the mass, and then he stood up straight and announced, "Butternuts! Nothing but butternuts! Young man, you pick up every single one and get that luggage back on the stagecoach."

The Flints stood and watched, while from the stagecoach came jeers and complaints. Timothy's hands shook as he picked up the nuts, but beside him he felt Henri, helping. He knew his face was red to his very ears.

"But I *know* they took the furs," Timothy said to Henri. To the sheriff he said, "Sir, this doesn't prove anything except that I was mistaken about the place. They've hidden them some place."

Surprisingly the sheriff was amenable.

"You give me the description of the furs, son," he said, "and I'll keep a lookout for them. Any way of identification?"

The Flints were all ears.

"Get back into the stage, you!" the sheriff thundered.

Henri, puzzled, followed the Flints inside. He was pleased that the sheriff was taking time to listen to Timothy, though the restive horses pawed the ground.

Riding slowly into the yard at the tannery, Timothy sat his mount mournfully. As he reached the barn, he slid off the horse, removed the bridle, and put Prince in his stall. Ash came out to meet him from the direction of the house.

"No furs?" he inquired, looking at Timothy's empty hands.

"No furs," Timothy answered. "I made a fool of myself into the bargain."

"Would it help you any," Ash inquired, "if I let you search around the tannery? Not that I think the peltries are here, but just to make you feel better."

"I'll never feel any better," Timothy decided.

Reaching home he confided his disappointment to Billy, who was working on the beaver pelts in the shed.

"It's never safe to jump to conclusions," Billy said quietly. "It was partly my fault this morning. I didn't listen when Rella mentioned the sled tracks either."

"Sled tracks?" Timothy demanded. "What have sled tracks to do with the loss of the furs?"

"That remains to be seen," Billy decided.

CHAPTER 9.

Sled Tracks

❖❖❖❖❖❖❖❖❖❖❖❖❖❖❖

IT WAS ONE of those misty mornings when the hoarfrost covered every leaf and weed, and hung in the
evergreen trees like filmy white blossoms. The clean
soft snow was not yet tracked down even on the
hill road, and Rella, coming out of the warm kitchen,
took a deep breath as she looked at the enchanted
countryside.

Billy and Timothy were cutting up a dry pine
tree that Johnny Sterling had dragged down from
the hillside the day before. Billy had chopped off
the smaller branches, piling them neatly against
the sheltered side of the woodshed with the twigs.
Timothy set the trunk into the sawhorse. The crosscut saw made a pleasant familiar buzz as the two
brothers worked it back and forth. Whenever it
struck a knot there was a clippety-clap.

In the yard orchard, close to the house, Rella discovered delicate little tracks made by wood mice.
The little creatures, going back and forth, had
woven a dainty chain. There were some larger, more
familiar tracks made by rabbits. Shep's footprints

told Rella that the collie had leaped as he ran. Doubtless he had chased the big white rabbit that loved to nibble the apple bark.

Rella ran out on the road to watch the stagecoach go by with its precious load of passengers and mail. The stage had turned along Front Street from Water Street. Now, coming up the hill, dragging the huge sled used by the tannery to haul small loads of hides to the levee freight office, was a tiny figure. It was Emma Murgner, the tanner's little girl.

Rella raced down the hill to meet her.

"Hello, Emma," she cried, and took vigorous hold of the rope. "Looks to me as if the sled should be pulling you, instead of your pulling the sled."

"It is heavy," Emma admitted, and gladly relinquished the rope.

"Am I going too fast?" Rella asked.

"No," said Emma. "Why are you dragging the sled along the side of the road? It goes much easier in the ruts."

"I know," Rella agreed, her thoughts racing.

Should she tell little Emma Murgner what she had told Billy yesterday morning—that she suspected the tracks in the snow had something to do with the stolen peltries? Now she wanted to prove whether this sled made wide tracks like the ones near the woodshed.

Emma was running to keep up, sometimes

stumbling in the ruts. Her sober blue eyes looked straight ahead as though she were watching the hoarfrost on the tall roadside trees that was beginning to fall like snow. Her thoughts must have been racing too.

"Rel-la," she panted, "I'm sor-ry about the pel-tries."

"Of course you are," Rella agreed. "Who do you think took them?"

"I don't know," Emma admitted.

The two little girls had reached the top of the hill. They sat down on the sled to rest. Rella asked, "Do you see the tracks your sled made in the snow?"

"Oh, yes." Emma laughed gleefully. "So that's why you ran it along the side of the road. It does make pretty tracks."

"Are there any other tracks like that in the whole of Reads Landing, do you think?" Rella inquired.

"There couldn't be," Emma explained, "because my father had Gus Stennerson, the blacksmith, forge those runners. He wanted them wide like that so they wouldn't sink in the slush when the loads of hides were heavy. They're lovely runners."

Rella hesitated only a moment before she said, "Emma, this sled was used to haul Billy's muskrat peltries away. It was this sled."

"It was this sled?" Emma repeated it with rising inflection. "How do you know?"

"Because the tracks that ran close beside our picket fence near the woodshed were wide like these," Rella answered. "They were exactly like these."

"How do you know?" Emma was puzzled. "The snow covered everything."

"They froze—the slush tracks did—before the snowstorm," Rella explained. "I imagine they're still frozen under the snow."

Billy and Timothy had finished their sawing and were splitting the chunks of wood into kitchen stove sizes. Their axes hit the hard blocks expertly. Rella called out, "Billy! Timothy! Come here a minute."

The boys both greeted Emma pleasantly as they walked over to the sled.

"What's happened?" Timothy inquired. "Rella, you have the look of a county sheriff about to disclose a find."

"I want to show you some sled tracks," Rella said. "I think they were made by this sled."

She walked over to the woodshed, and the others followed.

Emma stood quietly by while Billy and Timothy brushed away the new-fallen snow with their hands until they got down to the frozen sled tracks. Then Timothy ran to the kitchen doorway and brought over the old broom which was used for cleaning

snow or muddy shoes. Gently he swept the rest of
the snow from the ice.

"Well?" He leaned on the broom, raising his
eyebrows.

Neither Billy nor Rella, though they were bursting to speak, said a word.

Emma stared down at the frozen tracks. Here
and there Billy had broken off a piece of the rut,
but enough was left to show quite clearly the exact
shape of the runner that had made the track. Emma
bent and brushed away a little of the remaining
snow herself.

"It's our sled track all right," she admitted. "Our
runners made the ruts in the slush. But Ashley didn't
have anything to do with it. He'd never touch anything that didn't belong to him."

"No," Billy agreed. "Let's leave Ashley out of
this. But how about those two cousins of his?"

"They might." Emma nodded. "Or they might
not."

"Clear as mud," Timothy observed. "Emma, who
had a chance to borrow the sled besides Ashley and
the Flints?"

"Anybody," Emma answered. "Father always
tilts it up against the side of the barn, the runners
outward, so the top won't get snowy or wet."

"But I'd certainly think Ash would know about
it, if someone borrowed the sled," Timothy insisted.

Mrs. Dustin appeared in the kitchen doorway to ask Billy to pump her some fresh water, and heard what Timothy said. Handing the pail out, she saw that Emma was quite distraught. Wisely she offered no sympathy, because Emma was already on the verge of bursting into tears. She smoothed back her dark hair with the gesture that always told her children she was disturbed. Her full blue calico dress, with the tight, button-trimmed basque, crackled with starch as she turned briskly toward Rella.

"Rella, come in and help me peel apples for dumplings," she commanded. "Bring Emma in with you. Emma, I'm sure your mother won't mind lending you to me for one morning to help Rella."

"Oh, Mrs. Dustin," Emma said, shy but pleased.

"Timothy, please go to Duerre's and see if my ground cinnamon is ready," she continued in the same lively manner. "Go right on to the tannery from there and tell Mrs. Murgner I'm keeping Emma to dinner. Ashley can call for her this afternoon— say, around four."

"What's Mother's idea of bringing the enemy into camp?" Timothy murmured to Billy.

"Maybe she doesn't consider him an enemy. Maybe she agrees with Emma, that Ash is innocent."

"Let's not be too soft." Timothy tightened up.

"While I'm downtown, I'm going to report the sled tracks to Sheriff Young. He ordered me to report all clues."

"A good idea," Billy agreed. "But I wouldn't blat out my opinion of what the clues mean. You know what happened when you jumped to conclusions on the contents of the portmanteau."

"Can't you let me forget anything?" Timothy's face was red.

◇◇◇◇◇◇◇
◇◇◇◇◇◇◇

The sheriff was not in his office, but a stout young deputy sat with his legs on the desk.

"Got some new clues, Timothy?" he teased. "Something about butternuts or such like? Listen, Bub, you cain't tell a crook by his looks any more'n you kin tell a clue by hankerin' fer one. Take things easy-like, and them lost furs is apt to turn up in front o' yer eyes one of these days."

"I hope so," Timothy said and backed out of the office.

Timothy gave Mrs. Murgner his mother's message and then found Ashley in the barn, currying Prince. The boy turned as Timothy darkened the doorway, the curb straps still on his hands, that looked blue with cold.

"Message from my mother," Timothy announced.

"Emma's staying to dinner and Ma wants you should come by around four and pick her up."

Ashley looked surprised. There was no reason why Emma should not come home alone, and both boys knew it.

"All right," Ashley said quietly. "I'll come."

He looked hopefully at Timothy, but Timothy was already walking out of the yard.

The dinner was festive, made so by the addition of crab apple pickles, baking powder biscuits, and currant jelly that quivered in a fancy mold that had once been an odd dish. There was baked apple dumpling, served with thick cream.

About four o'clock Ashley knocked at the back door. He was so scrubbed that even the knuckles of his hands looked pink, and his fair hair, when he removed his cap, was plastered to his head. Billy and Timothy did not come in immediately, and Mrs. Dustin sent Mary out to tell them that Ashley had arrived.

"They couldn't help but see Ash from the wood-shed door," Mary objected, but her mother frowned her down.

At last Billy and Timothy came in, saying politely, "Hello, Ash."

Ashley, more direct, answered their unspoken thoughts.

"I've been thinking," he said, looking straight at

Timothy, "that we ought to start a search for Billy's peltries ourselves—not leave it just to the sheriff and his deputy. If I can catch up on my work, I'd like to hunt for them."

"Might be a good idea," Timothy answered.

Timothy watched Ashley depart with little Emma Murgner on the sled. Through the sitting room windows, his eyes stormy with anger, he watched the progress of the sled.

"Ash certainly knows how to hold that rope back up over Emma," he conceded, "and guide that sled so it won't slip downhill too fast!"

"Hold back on your opinions the way Ash is holding back on that sled, and we'll get results," Billy advised.

But Timothy's thoughts continued in a rut of his own making.

"Maybe he feels sorry he took the furs and will lead us to them," he mused. "Maybe he'll pretend to look for them and lead us to the cache."

Billy went out, slamming the door behind him.

CHAPTER 10.

The Wolf Pack

◈◈◈◈◈◈◈◈◈◈◈◈◈◈◈◈

ASHLEY KEPT HIS WORD by catching up with his work at the tannery. He and Mr. Murgner took down the last hides from the fence, counted, beat, and cleaned them, and packed them in bales. Ashley had the whole of Saturday free, and shortly after breakfast he appeared at the back door of the Dustin house. The Dustins were having their second cups of coffee, and Pierre, the Captain's old friend, who had brought a fine, cleaned sturgeon as a gift, was striving to persuade Mrs. Dustin that the fish was worth cooking. The old Frenchman's mustaches worked up and down.

"By gar," he was saying as Timothy admitted Ashley, "sturgeon is a sweet fish, ma'am. Good as pike any day."

Mrs. Dustin, with a stubborn glint in her violet-blue eyes, said, "I don't doubt your word, Pierre."

Pierre let his arms drop in dramatic fashion.

"All right, ma'am, give it away if you don't want it," he said. "I'll take my gun and go out and get you a pheasant. By gar, that you would like, eh?"

"Yes, pheasant is Permelia's favorite fish," the Captain declared and looked up. "Make a place for Ashley. How are you, my boy?"

Timothy managed to get in a word edgewise as Ashley made his desire known.

"Ash wants me to go up to Devil's Cave, Father," he said. "He thinks the peltries might have been hidden there. Indian Joe told him there were caches of furs made there in the early days."

Pierre squinted at Ashley through the clouds of pipe tobacco that enveloped his head like yellow storm clouds. "No gun?"

"Mr. Murgner asked me not to take it," Ashley explained. "There's a lot of tough climbing in the rocks up there, and Mr. Murgner's afraid of an accident."

"Murgner's right," the Captain agreed. "You'll need both hands free."

"I wish Billy were going along," Mrs. Dustin worried. "But I suppose it will take most of the day for him and Johnny Sterling to get the winter wood under cover. Billy's so reliable."

"You'd think I'd never been in the woods before," Timothy grumbled. "I can take care of myself."

"Caves are different from woods," Mrs. Dustin said. "Be sure to carry matches and candles."

"I have plenty of matches," Ashley assured her. "Mr. Murgner gave them to me in a tin box."

He slapped his coat pocket appreciatively.

"Don't fall through any holes in that cave," Mrs. Dustin warned. "Always look where you are going. Oh, my! I don't think that you should rightly go at all."

Even as she fussed, she began to spread great slices of bread thick with butter, to slide the left-over sausages in between, and to wrap a few dough-nuts in a napkin. Deftly she slipped apples into the boys' pockets.

"No need to worry, Mother." Captain Dustin looked dreamily out of the window to the hills, puffing at his tobacco and kinnikinnick. "I explored that cave often when I was a boy. It has a good, solid limestone floor, and there's a narrow passage-way in the back of the main cave that runs clear through the hill and comes out in a hazel copse above Beaver's Farm. Brush and trees have grown up around the opening. Guess the new generation isn't so adventuresome as we were."

"Now, William," Mrs. Dustin chided, "don't go encouraging Timothy to do anything dangerous. Make haste, son, or you won't get back before dark."

She put the packet of food into his hands, and he gave her a resounding smack. Rella and Mary followed him to the door and waved good-by as he and Ashley set out, their feet squeaking in the dry snow.

All over the town the white wood smoke rose straight into the clear air against the blue sky. It was frosty cold. Ashley kept covering his nose with his mittened hand or slapping his cheeks.

"Don't want to risk frostbite," he explained.

"Pull your wool scarf over your chin," Timothy advised, "and your cap down over your eyes and ears."

Timothy led the way across the gully beyond the Dustin house and bent forward to climb the steep, rocky sidehill towards the sheer bluffs overhanging the frozen Mississippi. Except for an occasional track of rabbit or deer, there was no indication that anything living had crossed the smooth snow.

From time to time the boys stopped to examine some strange rock formation that might prove to be a cache. The frosty rocks seemed piled in a wild jumble without direction, but towards afternoon, as he and Ashley proceeded slowly, Timothy became aware of something familiar in his surroundings. Something clicked in his memory. Once long ago Indian Joe had taken him to the Devil's Cave and they had gone on a trail.

"Just a minute, Ash!" Timothy called out. "I think there's an old Indian trail somewhere around here."

He recognized two immense rocks through which

he and Indian Joe had passed. They stood like guards to a path—and they were. Wedging himself between them, he set his feet upon a smooth, narrow path, protected by the other solid rocks from a rainfall of pebbles rolling from above.

Now they moved more swiftly, and Timothy, with that sure instinct that following trails all his boyhood had taught him, led the way out just below Devil's Cave. It was well past noon and they sat down to rest and to eat a sandwich. It was quite comfortable among the sunny rocks, shut off from the wind.

"Ash," Timothy mused, "did you ever see ermine so soft that it looked like milkweed down? And did you ever see sable or fox so silvery that it had a sheen like silver?"

"Where did you ever see anything like that?" Ashley inquired, mystified.

"At the Dousman house," Timothy answered. "Henri Derosia's sister had an ermine cape that might have belonged to a queen, and his mother had a sable scarf. The silver fox? Maybe I just dreamed that. But when I grow up, I'm going to make beautiful furs."

"You don't make furs," Ashley said dryly. "They grow on animals."

No use arguing with Ash. He knew hides but he did not know pelts. And assuredly he did not know the finished product of the artist—furs. Ash rose to his feet.

"Let's get up into the cave," he suggested. "The sun sets early these days."

Once off the Indian trail, the climbing was hard. With the small hatchet he carried in his belt, Ashley attempted to cut steps in the glare ice, but to no avail.

"Let's try the approach from the side. The Indian trail follows around there," Timothy suggested.

"Why didn't you say so in the first place?" Ashley grumbled.

An hour ago the bother of winding back and forth on an old Indian trail that had to be rediscovered in the snow would not have appealed to either impatient boy. But now the meandering trail, that took advantage of every crook and turn in the natural rock formation, seemed almost magical. Ashley reached out and gathered branches that stuck up out of the snow.

"What's the idea of loading yourself down with all that?" Timothy asked. "I'm sweating."

"Me too. But it will be nice to have a fire in the mouth of the cave," Ashley called back. "We can make toast, and those sausages won't be so greasy heated. Besides, it's fun."

"That's right," Timothy agreed and began to

collect wood, too. Every broken branch snapped like a shot in the cold air.

The boys flung themselves down on the floor of the cave, exhausted from the long, hard climb in the icy air. They piled the brush up and looked around. It was too cold and exposed in the open cave for any animal to take refuge there, though there might be bats hibernating in the ceiling far above them. The decline below was steep and perilous, and an unbroken expanse of snow continued down to the river. The bare oaks beyond the ice barrier rustled their dead leaves like old women shivering in brown silk. The outlook was so bleak that they turned back to the cave as if for comfort. Yet they shuddered at the small black mouth inside.

"No bear would choose a place like this," Timothy remarked. "Give me a nice warm little cave or a cozy hollow tree. I'm hungry. How about you? It must have taken us hours to make that climb."

"Let's light the fire." Ashley set a little bunch of twigs at the mouth of the cave and touched a match to them. They crackled up, making sparks that exploded in the cold air.

The boys kept adding wood, and began to toast bread on sticks, holding it near the embers that were red as coals. The butter sizzled with a pleasant sound and odor. If only they had gathered more wood!

Replete with food at last, Timothy lay on his stomach just inside the cave and munched an apple. Reads Landing looked very peaceful and lazy down there in the bottom of the bowl of hills. If only he could get back down there as the crow flies! He said as much to Ashley, whose eyes were on the closer view.

Instead of answering, Ashley made a sudden exclamation.

"Look!" He pointed with a shaking finger.

"Where?" Timothy asked wildly, catching the terror in Ashley's voice. "What are you talking about?"

But Ashley did not need to answer. Timothy himself saw. Behind a rock, down below them, crouched a shaggy form. It moved slightly forward for a better view, then retreated and waited, while Timothy caught his breath in a sharp spasm of fear. Even as he looked he perceived another behind another rock. He glanced sidewise at Ashley. He had seen them too. Now another pair became visible. Brush or timber wolves, whatever they were, they were reconnoitering as surely as though they were enemy soldiers. One wolf alone would have been cowardly, but they were rounding up in a pack for the kill.

Ashley's longing eyes were now on the village

below, where tiny squares of golden light began to pierce the soft gray darkness.

"If they come too close," Timothy said with determination, "we can throw lighted sticks at them. They're afraid of fire. Billy says so."

"We haven't much fuel," Ashley pointed out. "These little sticks won't last."

"You're right; they won't," Timothy agreed. "I'll get some wood."

Just then a wolf let out a weird, shuddering howl. Bold and determined, he advanced, looking up at the fire. Timothy seized the biggest stick in the fire and hurled it towards the ugly, shaggy form. The wolf retreated.

"See!" Timothy pointed out, his legs shaking. "See what cowards they are!"

The wolves waited. Soon another approached the fire, measuring the distance from below with his burning eyes. This time Ashley flung a brand.

The wolves would approach stealthily; then they would retreat, withdrawing behind the rocks—to wait.

Timothy squinted down at the semi-circle as it formed. The intermittent howling continued, each long-drawn-out spasm of horrible sound seeming to hang in the air. If the wind were right, that sound would carry into the village.

It was growing colder and darker now. Those eyes below began to glow in the deepening shadows.

"Ash," said Timothy, "I'm going through the cave to the other side of the bluff to get wood."

"I'm going with you!" Ashley announced.

"No. If we both went into the cave, the wolves would begin to try to leap up here. Or worse still, they might find the side paths. Listen, Ash, you must stay here and keep the fire burning. But don't waste a stick."

"All right, Timothy," Ash agreed. "But hurry!"

Timothy fled into the weirdly lighted cave. He plunged into the dark entrance that had seemed so fearsome in the afternoon. It was so low that he had to stoop and so narrow that he had to push himself along, feeling in front and crawling, kicking with his feet. In a short time, however, the passage widened up into a room in which he could stand. He stopped only long enough to light a match that showed the narrow opening to another tunnel ahead. He wedged his way into it, grateful that he could stand upright. He was conscious that the walls on either side of him—walls that pressed against his body, were soft. At any moment they might cave in on him. But at last he emerged into another hard limestone tunnel and now—now he could see stars ahead in the blue night sky, shining above the brush that covered the opening. His father's description was right. The cave did run way through the bluff.

The shuddering howls of the wolves on the other side of the bluff were faint but terrifying.

He broke long sticks, binding them together with his scarf so that he could drag them through the narrow passageways. His return was faster than he had dreamed it could be, especially after he had passed through the soft walls again. Now he could hear the howls of the pack and Ashley's wild yells of defiance.

Timothy dragged the wood into the open with a shout. The fire flamed up. The brands flew. But the wolves, their numbers augmented, were beginning to make running attempts to scale the icy slope. It was amazing how far they could jump. A few canny ones were lurking in the brush, nosing their way along the Indian trail that the boys had broken.

"If the worst comes to the worst," Timothy decided, "we'll both make a dash for the cave. They can't all follow us into the soft tunnel. We can defend ourselves against one with a sharp stick."

"The soft tunnel?" Ashley questioned, fearful in his terror that he had not heard aright.

But Timothy never answered him because at this moment there was a sharp crackling noise, different from anything else. A wolf howled, spun, and dropped.

"Gunfire!" Ashley yelled.

"Gunfire!" Timothy echoed.

CHAPTER 11.

The Cache

◆◆◆◆◆◆◆◆◆◆◆◆◆◆◆◆◆◆◆◆◆

ALL AFTERNOON, as Mrs. Dustin moved between stove and kitchen table, tending her crock of pork and beans, her apple and mince pies, and her browning loaves of bread, she fussed over Timothy's absence. Her mind on him, she made a dish of Indian pudding, his favorite dessert, and slid it into the already crowded oven. Isabel, lifting molasses cookies from a pan, said, "Timothy can take care of himself, Mother."

Even the Captain was restless. He cleaned his deer rifle and examined Billy's and Johnny's muskets, which had never failed to reveal shining barrels.

Towards dusk, as pheasants flew, Pierre stopped in at the Dustin house, proudly proffering a brace of handsome birds, their plump breasts beautifully speckled.

"Youngsters home yet?" he inquired. "Saw wolf tracks beyond the gully. Don't mean nothin', but, by gar, I don't like 'em."

"It's getting dark fast," Mrs. Dustin worried. "Set the table, Isabel, and call Rella and Mary in."

"Yes, Mother," Isabel said brightly. "Don't worry about the boys. They're probably on their way home now."

"If you're talking about Ash and Tim," Mary said dramatically as she came in with Rella, "they're *not* on their way home yet."

"They have a fire burning in front of Devil's Cave," Rella explained, "and they always put fires out before they leave a camp."

"Timothy never did have any sense of time," Mrs. Dustin complained. "Father, I think someone should go after him."

"Now, Permelia," Captain Dustin said soothingly, "you know how hard it is for a boy to leave a campfire. He'll be along."

Isabel lit the lamps. As she pulled the chain of the kerosene parlor lamp with its cheerful red roses, she thought, It's extravagant to light this too, but the more guiding light the better for the boys. The gold from the parlor windows made a path over the unsullied snow to the gully.

When she returned to the kitchen, the Captain was urging Pierre to have a bite with the family. Billy and Johnny Sterling had just come in, bringing in the frost on jackets and caps. Their cheeks were very red, their eyes bright.

"Below zero," Billy reported.

"And steadily dropping," Johnny added; then,

his bright hazel eyes meeting Isabel's, he said, "We're as hungry as wolves."

Mrs. Dustin shivered, and Johnny, always sensitive to the least change in the family atmosphere, wondered what he had said or done that was amiss.

Usually Saturday night supper was cheerful in the Dustin house, but tonight even Rella's blue eyes were anxious as she poured cream on her Indian pudding. Mary kept watching the door, listening for the creak of returning footsteps.

Isabel had purposely delayed the serving of the corn pudding, as everybody knew, hoping that the two boys would arrive to enjoy their belated supper. Perhaps, she suggested, they had left the fire burning at the mouth of the cave to light their way down among the rocks. No danger of fire spreading in all that ice and snow!

When steps finally did creak in the dry snow, Mrs. Dustin got to her feet, her face lighted with gladness. Johnny smiled across the table at Isabel. Rella and Mary clasped hands, and Billy exchanged an understanding look with his father. Pierre continued to eat; although his eyes seemed to be only on his pudding, his whole attitude was alert.

But the door was not flung open. Somebody knocked timidly. Billy, who was closest, jumped to his feet and jerked the door open. There stood Mr. Murgner, his old musket in one hand, his lantern in the other. It was Emma who had knocked. Her eyes were bright pools of light in her small face.

Mr. Murgner said, "When I went out to bed down Prince, I heard the howl of wolves. Sound comes down the draw to my place, you know, from the caves up on the hill. Emma heard me telling Mother, and nothing would do but she must come along."

He held the door open, and a faint, curdling howl rushed in with the bitter cold, crowding out the food-fragrant warmth of the kitchen. Mrs. Dustin and Isabel grew pinched and white-looking. Pierre, wiping his mouth with the back of his hand, pushed his chair back and stepped out into the snow. Then he stepped swiftly back again.

"Don't you worry, ma'am," he said. "The fire just flamed brighter'n ever. Dead boys don't make fires, and wolves ain't smart enough."

"Thank you, Pete," Mrs. Dustin breathed.

Billy and Johnny got into their jackets and caps again and checked their ammunition. The Captain moved spryly.

All of the menfolk, followed by Mr. Murgner, rushed down through the snowy gully and up over the hill where the wind had swept the snow clean. Pierre was far ahead, rushing along even where the snow was deeper among the weeds and brambles.

◇◇◇◇◇◇
◇◇◇◇◇◇

It was Pierre's shot that Timothy and Ashley heard as they crouched on the cliff in front of the mouth of the cave. The first shot was followed by others as the rest of the party arrived.

The hungry pack scattered, running swiftly toward the ravine for shelter. But one giant wolf, probably the leader of the pack, turned back snarling, reluctant to leave the prey. His fiery eyes glared at the group advancing through the snowy weeds and rocks. His long, gaunt form rose to the edge of the gully.

"By gar, I get heem!" Pierre shouted as he slid over the ice that had thawed and frozen as it dripped from the cave.

As the rifle shot rang out, the giant wolf leaped into the air and then lay stretched out on the reddening snow.

Mr. Murgner caught one sly, small wolf working his way up the Indian trail towards the boys.

"Mr. Murgner!" Ashley yelled, his voice breaking on a sob.

"Billy! Johnny! Father!" Timothy exulted.

He could say no more, he was so relieved that he felt weak. His voice died away, and his sturdy legs that had held him up so valiantly gave way. He sank down on the cliff beside Ashley.

"How did you get up there?" Captain Dustin shouted. "Fly?"

"Wish we could have," Timothy managed to say, feeling life flowing back into him. "We came by the old Indian trail."

"Put out your fire and come back down the same way," Captain Dustin ordered.

"Let me hold onto you, Tim, going down," Ashley whispered.

"All right, Ash," Timothy agreed, "if you'll let me hold onto you."

◆◆◆◆◆◆◆
◆◆◆◆◆◆◆

Emma helped Mary and Rella set the table a second time while they waited for the men and boys to return. The fire was out on Devil's Cave hill.

Then they all came in with shouting and laughter, and Timothy was being scolded and consoled at one and the same time.

"There'll be no more searching." Mrs. Dustin laid down the law even while she rejoiced over the wolf pelts, five of them and all handsome. "I don't want to hear the word 'cache' ever again."

"Forget about it, Tim," Johnny Sterling advised, pouring himself a cup of coffee just to be sociable. "If you have a nightmare, I'll wake you up."

"But I don't want to forget about it," Timothy announced, his eyes suddenly bright. "Father, were you always as stout as you are now?"

"Just about," the Captain boasted. "I was one of those youngsters who never went through the thinning stage."

"Then there was plenty of room for you when you crawled through the cave?"

"Plenty. Why do you ask that?"

"Because I've got an idea."

"I've got an idea too," Billy put in. "You and Ash are going to have a present of the wolf peltries."

"No wolves for me," Ash decided. "Mr. Murgner may have my share. Thanks just the same."

"If you're going into the fur business with me, Ash," Timothy teased, "you'll have to learn to meet up with wolves."

"I'll run the tannery end," Ashley decided.

"And I'll help you," Emma offered.

"I'll wear the furs," Rella announced, and Mary added, "Me too!"

"Mother, please don't tell me not to mention a cache again." Timothy looked up from his plate into Mrs. Dustin's blue eyes, still concerned for him. "Because, Mother, *I think I've found one.*"

"What are you talking about?" Captain Dustin asked sharply. "You'd better go to bed and talk things over after a good night's rest. Those wolves have given you fancies."

"Please listen, all of you." Timothy's eyes swept the group imploringly.

Every face turned toward him as Timothy went over the account of his experiences in the cave and particularly in the passageway that seemed to have the strangely soft walls.

"Both times," he said, "in spite of being scared to death, I noticed the walls. They felt more like cloth than soil. How could there be soft soil? There's not a single drop of water. I never saw such a dry cave."

Everybody was quiet, absorbed in his own thoughts.

"Nobody would have bothered to carry sixty muskrat pelts up there," Billy decided. "They wouldn't be worth the bother."

"I don't think it is the muskrat pelts," said Timothy. "Even if they'd stuffed them into sacks, there wouldn't be enough to fill two sides of that passageway."

"Maybe it's just bedding—gunny sacks stuffed with straw—used by early settlers hiding from the Indians," Ashley mused. "That passageway would have been safe to sleep in because it couldn't be seen from the mouth."

"And it may be all Tim's imagination," Johnny Sterling said, but his voice showed his excitement. "I suggest we all take next Saturday off and investigate."

"Are the passageways like catacombs?" Emma inquired. "There's a picture in our history."

"With candles set in niches," Rella said.

"And piles of bones," Mary added.

"No bones," Timothy informed her dryly. "But the candle idea is a good one. We could set candles in niches."

"Lanterns are more practical," Johnny Sterling decided. "If there really is soft dirt in that passageway, I'll take along a shovel to dig you out, Tim."

"Only you won't be so much of a hero, Tim, this next time," Billy teased. "No wolves."

"There won't be any next time," Mrs. Dustin put in.

"Tell you what, Permelia," the Captain said, "we'll send Johnny and Billy to investigate and leave Timothy and Ashley at home."

A furor rose about the table.

As the week went by Mrs. Dustin, catching the spirit of the adventure as her fears quieted, no longer offered objections. She mended Timothy's blanket coat to wear over his deerskin tunic and leggings. Isabel added some red wool to the cap she was knitting for him. "So you'll look like a voyageur with a red kerchief on your head," she explained.

Mrs. Dustin laughed with Isabel.

"I ought to put up a voyageur's lunch for them," she said, "hulled corn, smoked venison, some bear fat, and a little maple sugar."

"In a birch-bark basket," Isabel suggested. "We provide the setting. The boys will have to do the rest."

As the four boys left the Dustin kitchen on Saturday morning, each one carrying a lantern along with shovels and pickaxes and an ample lunch, Timothy added another bit of information he had not mentioned before. It was not that he had forgotten it, but he had not been quite sure.

"I thought I smelled cedar in that narrow passageway," he said, as he waded through the deep drifts. "I was almost smothered, and when I caught my breath, the odor of cedar was strong. I didn't think much about it then, but I remember it."

"That's not important, is it?" Johnny Sterling asked, climbing up through the gully behind Billy.

"Yes, it is," Billy called back, "because furs were often packed in cedar or covered with the boughs. Cedar makes a good cover to keep off rain because the branches are flat and lace together well, and it keeps its smell for years."

Ashley, who was walking ahead with Timothy,

turned around. "I suppose it seems years since you lost your muskrat pelts, Billy."

Timothy said, "Let's not talk muskrats; we're out for bigger game."

He led the way, walking fast in spite of the climb. Like an Indian he wedged his way through weeds and rocks until he found the Indian trail. Everybody followed him swiftly in single file.

The climb along the Indian trail in the bright sunlight was much easier. It seemed to Timothy and Ashley that they knew every scrub and juniper root by which to help themselves along.

The blackened ashes of the fire on the cliff still held half-burnt twigs. The wolves were only a bad dream.

Billy strode into the outer cave with Johnny, and the two young men cut a good solid niche in the limestone, wide enough to hold a lantern. In the smaller tunnels Timothy and Ashley made little niches to hold candles. Timothy had insisted on the candles, so that the entire cave formation could be seen. Now they were ready to make a careful examination of the so-called soft tunnel.

The four crowded in one after the other, Timothy and Ashley followed by Billy and Johnny. They examined the cold walls with their hands. Everything in the narrow tunnel was covered with at least an inch of finely powdered limestone.

"No erosion would have sprinkled the stuff so evenly," Billy pronounced. "It *is* a cache."

"The walls are made up of one bag piled onto another," Johnny Sterling exclaimed, coughing in the dust his investigation raised. "Let's drag these things into the main cave. Then we can look them over."

Timothy understood now what had kept him from getting through the tunnel easily. Bags were piled on either side, covered first with flat sprays of cedar and then with a layer of powdered limestone.

As Billy jerked his first bag down to the floor of the tunnel, a cloud of dust filled the air. The boys all choked on the mingled powder of limestone and cedar so old and dry that it went to pieces at a touch, though it still retained its fragrance.

There were twelve bales that the boys dragged into the main cave, lighted from the outside by sunlight gleaming on the snow and on the inside by the lantern making a glow on the limestone walls.

Billy's hands were shaking in his excitement as he tried to unlace the rawhide thongs.

Suddenly Timothy shouted from the tunnel, "Come here, Billy. Quick!"

Johnny Sterling took down the lighted lantern

and brought it in so that the boys could all get a good view. The first layer of bales had been removed in practical darkness. Now the lighted lantern showed poles set into the rock, each pole the length of the short passageway. Timothy's sensitive hands had been following them. The ends rested in niches cut to fit them.

Across these poles had been placed pieces of birch bark and under them were more pieces of the white, clean bark. There was a scent of cedar, too, but there was no powdered limestone.

"The furs in the bales below are so valuable," Timothy reasoned, "that whoever placed them here placed the poles so that the furs wouldn't be matted from the weight above. These are the valuable furs all right."

"There are twelve bales," Ashley counted, "and there were twelve in the first layer. That makes twenty-four bales in all."

"Twenty-four bales!" Billy sounded wildly excited.

"What does that mean?" asked Johnny Sterling.

"There were twenty-four bales in the Ferguson shipment," Billy explained, "according to Gerald."

"This is the Ferguson fortune!" Timothy declared. "It must be. We've found the Ferguson fortune!"

"Jumping to conclusions as usual," Billy chided his brother.

For once Timothy accepted his brother's reproof without backing down.

"Maybe so," he conceded, "but don't you hope my guess is right?"

CHAPTER 12.

The Captain Consults with Gerald

◆◆◆◆◆◆◆◆◆◆◆◆◆◆◆◆◆◆

WHEN MRS. DUSTIN baked her pumpkin pies for Thanksgiving, she baked an extra pie with a covered crust. Its curved slits and fork marks oozed rich, dark juice.

"The last blueberry pie of the season," she announced to the Captain as he sat smoking beside the stove. "Double thick."

"For Indian Joe?" the Captain inquired, twinkling.

"For the family," Mrs. Dustin assured him, "though I shouldn't be one whit surprised if Indian Joe appeared. He seems to have an uncanny sense for locating blueberry pie. . . . By the way, William, where are you storing all those bales? I don't want them in my woodshed. Every time I go out there, I have to crowd past them."

"Don't the boys bring in the kindling wood?" the Captain inquired. "And don't I do pretty well when they're gone?"

"I don't want the responsibility of those furs,"

Mrs. Dustin confessed. "If thieves could take Billy's peltries, they could take these."

"It would be quite a take," the Captain reminded his wife. "Twenty-four bales, weighing at least a hundred pounds apiece! You know what a task it was just to get them down here."

"Yes, I know," Mrs. Dustin agreed, "but I don't understand why you don't open the bales and check things. Must you wait for Gerald?"

"I believe you yourself suggested that," the Captain said dryly.

She nodded.

Since that first day in the cave, when Johnny Sterling had unlaced the rawhide thongs that bound the first bale and discovered a pack of soft-skinned otter peltries, he and the Dustins had decided to keep the other bales intact until they could bring Gerald Ferguson down to Reads Landing for a view of what they hoped and believed would turn out to be the Ferguson cache.

The deep snow had prevented anybody's getting through the two miles between the Landing and Sanborn's Point. Even the stage had not been able to travel the St. Paul road for a week.

The Dustin boys, with Johnny Sterling, were joyously snowed in, building a shack on the bottoms where they were cutting wood for the late winter. Isabel, Mary, and Rella had gone to stay for a few days with their married sister. It was Thanksgiving vacation.

It was rare for the Captain and Mrs. Dustin to be alone. The Captain, standing at the kitchen window that faced towards the snowy hills, gave a sudden chuckle.

" 'Speak of the devil and he's sure to appear,' " he quoted.

Mrs. Dustin went to stand beside her husband. Shading her eyes with her hand, she peered up into the white expanse. Flying along down the hill on snowshoes came Indian Joe.

" 'Speak of angels,' " she countered, " 'and you hear the flutter of their wings.' "

Her smile challenged the Captain, for Indian Joe did appear to be coming on winged feet.

"I'm going to hire Indian Joe to make me a pair of those snowshoes," the Captain decided. "They say he uses caribou instead of rawhide for the lacings. Caribou tends to shrink instead of stretch, and that keeps the shoes tight. Then that peak that turns up at the front is pretty nice. No chance of up-ending. See how he skims over the snow!"

"It isn't only the laces or the shape of the tips that helps Indian Joe to skim the snow," Mrs. Dustin mused. "He comes of a long line of people who have sped over the snow like gulls over water."

"Well, I come from a long line of people whose

boats have sailed over the waves," the Captain
boasted. "No reason why I shouldn't snowshoe suc-
cessfully!"

He looked at the clear, cloudless sky, the sparkling white snow, and the frost hanging in the trees
like flowers.

"It's clearing," he announced. "Indian Joe can
take my message to Gerald."

◇◇◇◇◇◇
◇◇◇◇◇◇

Indian Joe set his snowshoes against the house
and came in, without knocking. He said, "How!"

"How!" Mrs. Dustin gave the word the proper
grunt and indicated a chair at the table. "Hungry?"

It was noon, dinner time in the village.

Indian Joe never failed to impress the Dustins by
his tallness and his grace. The bronze of his face
was like clear, polished metal. His eyes were dark
and searching, yet kindly. His black hair was bound
with red wool. Even his ill-fitting buckskin trousers
and jacket could not conceal the finely muscled
straightness of his body. He was no longer young,
yet he was childlike in his delight over any little
gift of food or trinket.

He ate his noon meal with the Captain and his
wife quietly. It was not until the giant wedge of

CHAPTER 12.

The Captain Consults with Gerald

◆◆◆◆◆◆◆◆◆◆◆◆◆◆◆◆◆◆

WHEN MRS. DUSTIN baked her pumpkin pies for Thanksgiving, she baked an extra pie with a covered crust. Its curved slits and fork marks oozed rich, dark juice.

"The last blueberry pie of the season," she announced to the Captain as he sat smoking beside the stove. "Double thick."

"For Indian Joe?" the Captain inquired, twinkling.

"For the family," Mrs. Dustin assured him, "though I shouldn't be one whit surprised if Indian Joe appeared. He seems to have an uncanny sense for locating blueberry pie. . . . By the way, William, where are you storing all those bales? I don't want them in my woodshed. Every time I go out there, I have to crowd past them."

"Don't the boys bring in the kindling wood?" the Captain inquired. "And don't I do pretty well when they're gone?"

"I don't want the responsibility of those furs,"

Mrs. Dustin confessed. "If thieves could take Billy's peltries, they could take these."

"It would be quite a take," the Captain reminded his wife. "Twenty-four bales, weighing at least a hundred pounds apiece! You know what a task it was just to get them down here."

"Yes, I know," Mrs. Dustin agreed, "but I don't understand why you don't open the bales and check things. Must you wait for Gerald?"

"I believe you yourself suggested that," the Captain said dryly.

She nodded.

Since that first day in the cave, when Johnny Sterling had unlaced the rawhide thongs that bound the first bale and discovered a pack of soft-skinned otter peltries, he and the Dustins had decided to keep the other bales intact until they could bring Gerald Ferguson down to Reads Landing for a view of what they hoped and believed would turn out to be the Ferguson cache.

The deep snow had prevented anybody's getting through the two miles between the Landing and Sanborn's Point. Even the stage had not been able to travel the St. Paul road for a week.

The Dustin boys, with Johnny Sterling, were joyously snowed in, building a shack on the bottoms where they were cutting wood for the late winter. Isabel, Mary, and Rella had gone to stay for a few blueberry pie was set before the guest that Captain Dustin stated the favor he wished.

"Joe, I want you to take a message to Gerald Ferguson at Sanborn's Point. Think you can get through?"

Indian Joe disdained to answer the question.

"Why Gerald not come back Ferguson house?" he inquired, knowing how much more comfortable the Ferguson family would be in Reads Landing instead of Sanborn's Point.

"Many time Chippewa change camp, something bad happen," Mrs. Dustin reasoned, speaking in the childlike language she had so often used with Indian Joe.

"Good house," Indian Joe said stolidly.

"Good house, bad memory," Mrs. Dustin replied.

The Captain broke in with the news of the finding of the cache by Timothy and Ashley. Indian Joe listened with a serene expression. Only the lighting of his eyes betrayed his real interest. But when the Captain cried, "We must get word to Gerald as soon as possible," Indian Joe jumped to his feet.

"Get word by sundown," he announced.

"Roads are bad," the Captain reminded the Indian.

"Two miles, crow flies," Indian Joe said. "Go like crow flies."

"If you're going, I want you to take something to

the Fergusons," Mrs. Dustin said, and began to bustle about packing a basket.

"Indian Joe no squaw," the messenger protested. Nevertheless he went off carrying his burden.

The next day just before noon Gerald Ferguson appeared, as tall and lithe as Indian Joe. Entering the Dustin kitchen, he tensely announced that he had borrowed his Indian friend's snowshoes for the trip and had left Indian Joe to look out for his family.

"I understand, Captain," he said, almost at once, "that you think you have found my father's furs. I can't quite believe it."

He spoke as though his throat were tight. There was a look in his face, a look of hope, that made Mrs. Dustin turn away to busy herself at the stove. In her heart rose a prayer for him.

"You can't quite believe it, eh?" Mrs. Dustin was glad that the Captain could tease Gerald and thus relieve the tension. "What makes you think the furs aren't yours even before you see them?"

"A good many furs were cached in those days," Gerald reasoned miserably. "Traders feared Indians and fur thieves. Sometimes there were delays caused by sickness when canoes had to be lightened and journeys hastened. It wasn't at all unusual to use caves as caches."

Even as he spoke, he was on the heels of the Captain, hurrying into the woodshed to look over the bales.

The Captain got down to business, and some of his calm affected Gerald. Still he could not wholly relax.

"The fewer people who know about the furs now the better," the Captain said. "Fortunately Permelia and I are at home alone these few days, and the snow makes neighboring difficult. There has already been too much talk."

"I understand so, sir." Gerald's sharp, bright glance flashed over the bales. "I was only a youngster at the time these bales were made up, but they look like ours." He swallowed hard, adding, "Maybe they just look like ours because I want them to. And the number is the same—twenty-four."

"Final judgment would have to be passed by the Dousman people and by Mr. Richards Gordon of St. Paul, I imagine," Captain Dustin said briskly.

"Mr. Gordon was to have made up two of the bales for royalty in Europe," Gerald remembered. "I can still hear my mother talking about it. Yes, Mr. Gordon would certainly recognize the two special bales that are earmarked." He pulled himself up sharply. "But then other traders may have used similar markings."

"Gerald, you're bending over backwards," Captain Dustin scolded.

"I know it," the young man acknowledged. "It's only because I couldn't stand the disappointment if it turns out that the furs aren't mine. When you've dreamed for twelve years of something you wish for more than anything else in the world, you have a hard time believing your dreams have come true. It would mean so much to Mary and to the children's future."

"Right now," the Captain said, "our job is to find a suitable cache where the furs will be safe until we can get them to St. Paul. We don't want to attract attention."

"We must not." Gerald's jaw set. "I couldn't stand losing them again, if they *are* mine. There's a ring of fur thieves operating in the bluffs around here, and this cache is rich enough to make them take any kind of chance."

As he spoke, he drew forth several pelts and stroked them with shaking hands.

The two men talked far into the night. Even a cursory examination had convinced them that the twenty-four bales were worth a king's ransom. They agreed that the two bales marked with colored threads and seals should remain intact. Where and how were the furs to be hidden?

At breakfast Mrs. Dustin said, "Being a woman, I'm naturally curious, but I'd just as lief you two didn't tell me where you are taking the furs. If I don't know, it won't hurt me and I won't be tempted to spread the news. For this would be news!"

She urged more cakes upon Gerald.

"Permelia, you always did keep a close mouth," the Captain said. "But have it your own way."

Gerald saw that he was pleased.

"It's beginning to snow again," Mrs. Dustin observed. "That will help to shut out prying eyes. In another day or two this household will be running normally again, with everybody home and neighbors running in. *Now* is the time."

The Captain patted his wife's shoulder as he rose.

"Come sundown, Permelia, we'll have the bales out of your woodshed, Providence permitting," he promised.

Mrs. Dustin hummed as she worked about the house. The world outside was a deep, white silence. The pines looked like giant white cones, and chimney smoke rose straight in white plumes above the mushroom houses.

Once she thought she heard sleigh bells, and a little later there came a tapping at the kitchen door.

She admitted Mr. Murgner, the tanner, who came in to warm his hands at the kitchen stove.

"Just came up with Prince to break the hill road," he said.

Mrs. Dustin poured him a cup of coffee and set a plate of doughnuts in front of him.

"I imagine Gerald went down on Indian Joe's snowshoes to get you up here," she guessed.

Mr. Murgner grinned broadly. "Mrs. Dustin," he said, "you're a smart woman."

There was a great deal of activity all day long in the woodshed, and the Murgner sledge made several trips down the hill. At dinner, around the noon hour, Gerald was full of praise for Prince.

"He certainly knows how to open roads," said Gerald.

"He's opened many a road," Mr. Murgner boasted. "The hill road is rather high, but the wind helps to keep it clear. There are no deep drifts like those on Water and Richards Streets."

Mrs. Dustin listened to this talk that led nowhere but away from the matter that concerned them all.

At supper time Mr. Murgner did not appear, although Mrs. Dustin had set a place for him. Snow still fell as early twilight came on, and every track of man or beast was covered. Gerald, looking a little worried, said, "Mr. Murgner says you can't see the river a hand's distance away."

"I don't need to see it," Captain Dustin boasted. "I know my river the way you know your cabin trail. And the job's almost done."

"I know that," Mrs. Dustin observed tersely. "When I stepped out for a breath of air, after Mr. Murgner's last trip, I noticed only two bales left behind, the ones with the pitch-pine seals and colored threads."

"For a breath of air!" The Captain looked at his wife reprovingly, and they all laughed.

"Don't forget to return Mr. Murgner's sled to him, William," Mrs. Dustin added. "You borrowed it to bring that quarter of beef up, remember?"

"Well!" the Captain exclaimed and said no more.

He and Gerald got into their heavy coats and caps again and pulled on their mittens, that had been drying near the stove over a chair back. Their cheeks were red and their eyes sparkled.

Mrs. Dustin washed her dinner dishes quickly. As she worked she left the door ajar, so that the soft snow wind freshened up the steamy room. But when she heard the voices of Gerald and the Captain and knew that they had come out of the woodshed, she flung the door open suddenly, to make a path of golden light for them to see by. The two bales had been roped to the sled.

"Breath of air, Mrs. Dustin?" inquired the Captain, his hand on the bales to steady them as Gerald picked up the rope.

"Breath of air," she acknowledged.

She watched them wading through the deep, sparkling snow until the white curtain shut them from sight. She almost wished she were in on the secret of the hiding place for the furs.

CHAPTER 13.

The Hard Moon

◆◆◆◆◆◆◆◆◆◆◆◆◆◆◆◆◆◆◆◆

By the first week in January the roads were open again, and the tinkling sounds of sleigh bells on harnesses and cutters were heard. Even the big horses that drew the Duerre grocery-laden freight lifted their great heads to a silvery jingle.

The Christmas trees shed their needles in the parlors and sitting rooms of Reads Landing, and soon all the holiday greenery had disappeared as fuel for fireplaces and stoves, giving out its last aromatic fragrance. Women grumbled, "No matter how much you sweep, you find needles in everything, from the children's clothes to the horse-hair upholstery cushions."

The children, back in school after Christmas vacation, settled down to their studies. During recess they watched the men cutting the lighter river ice, though they longed for Saturdays when the lake ice was being cut. The big boys could help on Saturdays.

"'As the days begin to lengthen, then the cold

begins to strengthen,' " Captain Dustin quoted, and it was certainly true.

The Indians called January the Hard Moon, and indeed the moon did look hard, hard as ice up there in the wintry sky. Down through the hills sometimes the villagers heard the howl of a wolf, but no one saw him. Perhaps, said Pierre, it might be the white wolf, the color of snow, the lucky white wolf that would bring fame and fortune to the hunter who shot him. But on these days Pierre chose to smoke his pipe in the Union House or in Duerre's store.

Mary, home from school one bitter January day, was talking to her mother as she cleaned the canary cage.

"Everybody says the cache Timothy and Ashley found couldn't have amounted to much," she reported.

"Who is everybody?" Mrs. Dustin inquired.

"Just everybody," Mary answered. "At recess all the big boys were making fun of Timothy and Ashley—said they weren't as smart as they thought they were."

"Very few people are as smart as they think they are," Mrs. Dustin said. "What did Timothy and Ashley do?"

"I was pretty proud of Tim," Mary said, as she cut a round from the smoothed store paper for the bottom of the cage. "Tim kept his temper."

Rella had come in. Now she stood at the table, poking a small, red finger at the canary sitting on his perch. He pecked at her and she squealed. Then he fluttered down to the lukewarm water in a dish that Mrs. Dustin set under the cage and began to flutter in it.

"Tim's keeping his temper is news," Mrs. Dustin said dryly. "How about Ashley?"

It was seldom that Mrs. Dustin pursued a subject, and the little girls were delighted.

"Ashley just looked embarrassed," Mary said with a short laugh. "He can't take teasing like Timothy."

"Mother," Rella inquired, "is it true that what we thought was the Ferguson cache didn't amount to anything—that it was just a bunch of old hides mostly and some straw bedding?"

"Whatever gave you such an idea?" Mrs. Dustin asked.

"Oh, some of the girls," Rella answered. "You know how those things are—somebody starts a story that something isn't good, and then it gets worse and worse."

"Yes, I know," said Mrs. Dustin. "Now make haste and get your good school clothes changed. Look! That bird is spattering right through the cage wires on your pinafore. I want you to go down to

Duerre's store for me. With all the menfolk on the ice, I declare there's no one to do an errand."

◆◆◆◆◆◆◆
◆◆◆◆◆◆◆

The river ice was thin, but at Sanborn's Point it had frozen to a thickness of a foot and a half and in some places two feet! The cold wind swept down over the thirty-mile length of Lake Pepin and came across the three-mile width at the Point with fury. But the road between Reads Landing and Sanborn's Point had been broken, and Gerald's log cabin, set in the valley between the protecting hills, looked almost snug.

The cabin became headquarters where the ice cutters dried their clothes and ate their noon meals. Johnny Sterling and Billy Dustin had taken a contract to provide Mr. Burkhardt with his season's ice for his meat market, and they had also agreed to fill the Wilson icehouse.

The Ferguson cabin, with bedroom at one end and kitchen at the other, was as gay as the turkey red curtains that hung at the windows. Mary Ferguson had a talent for home-making. She cooked hearty noon meals, pork and beans that had been baking in the oven overnight, or great kettles of boiled dinner—venison with cabbage, onions, potatoes, and rutabagas that she and Gerald had grown on new land. Mrs. Dustin sent frozen mince pies to her to help out and she heated them good and hot. They smelled rich and spicy, and they helped to fill the chinks in the hearty outdoor appetites of Gerald, Billy, and Johnny Sterling.

Little Joe would toddle from one knee to another, and his younger sister, Mary, would pound on her highchair tray with the porridge spoon that had been her christening gift from the Dustins. But Mary Ferguson was the heart of the house, pretty even in a faded red dress. Her dark eyes sparkled no matter how weary she was, and her wealth of black hair, braided and pinned like a chignon to the back of her shapely head, was always neat. Her soft voice was at once tender and gay. If at times her gaiety faltered, it was due to her concern for Gerald, so thin and workworn.

The days were still short, and the young men were out in the blue dawn, always at work when the first rosy light of the sun danced out over the snow.

Mr. Burkhardt would arrive to mark off the section to be cut. He was a big, heavy-set man with Nordic blue eyes, and he hardly stopped smoking his pipe long enough to give his orders. Sometimes he took one of the single saws and sent it whizzing through the ice, but he soon tired of the hard work and went back to the Landing in the cutter in which he had arrived.

Gerald invariably used a single saw to cut out the section to be handled, and Billy and Johnny used the crosscut saw to divide it into smaller pieces. The workers came to love the whirring, smooth rhythm with an occasional high note, so different from the uneven grating of wood cutting.

Dragging the blocks up onto the ice was usually Billy's job. He wore spiked shoes and wielded a fifteen-foot pike pole with which he edged the floating blocks onto the smooth surface of the ice. Once an edge of a huge block tilted up, the other young men seized the advantage and cut into it with tongs. Billy could "ride the ice" as expertly as he could ride a floating log. When the chunks were securely on the ice or the snowy shore, they were sawed into pieces of the proper size for loading.

Mr. Burkhardt provided a wide bobsled drawn by two gray draft horses for transporting the ice from the lake to his icehouse behind his market. Johnny engineered the piling of the ice cakes, three layers high, on the bobsled, whose poles creaked with the burden of holding the load.

Frequently the horses could not get started up the slope, and Gerald would run to the cabin for a pan of wood ashes to provide traction for the great hoofs. Only too often it took all three young men to get the huge ice cakes up the plank from the surface to the bobsled. Johnny would stand on top and reach down with his ice tongs, while Billy and Gerald held the cake steady with their own tongs.

Once started up the slope onto the road, the horses walked along without seeming strain and the boys could go back to work again.

All week long the great Burkhardt bobsled, its poles creaking, moved between Sanborn's Point and Reads Landing, the workers taking turns driving. The big grays, their heads down and the muscles of their thick necks swelling, would pull the bobsled to the icehouse back of the market. There was always someone to run in and tell Mr. Burkhardt, and he, in turn, would look up his roustabouts who had been hired to put the ice in, along with the sawdust packing. Mr. Burkhardt always grumbled when he went to look for his helpers.

"Swapping yarns!" he would shout. "Let them finish and the ice would melt."

The men wore mackinaws and heavy wool pants, and their red flannel underwear showed at their wrists as they clawed into the ice blocks with huge tongs, sliding them up on a wide plank to the helper above, who shoveled the proper amount of sawdust between cakes.

Pierre, smoking his pipe as he watched, would

remark, "By gar, some day that Billy he cut a block beeg like a house."

This year Timothy and Ashley had secured the sawdust job. Every day after school they took Prince and went to the mill at the edge of town, bringing up wagonloads of clean, fresh sawdust which they dumped beside the icehouse. A wagon-box had been set on runners, and Prince pulled the loads easily.

❖❖❖❖❖❖❖
❖❖❖❖❖❖

The Dustins had not finished breakfast on the third Saturday morning in January before Ashley appeared. He accepted a doughnut, but he kept looking at Timothy, ill at ease. Finally he said, "Mr. Murgner thought maybe you and I could ride up with Billy on the Burkhardt sled and work at the Point today instead of hauling sawdust. Mr. Burkhardt says there's enough there to last several days."

"Of course we can," Timothy said. "Does Mr. Murgner want to use Prince for something else?"

"Yes, I guess so," Ashley said.

Ashley was more quiet than usual on the ride to Sanborn's Point. He and Timothy stood behind Billy and Johnny Sterling, who sat on the high seat of the sledge. This was his first ice-cutting job.

Once he had arrived, he was fascinated by the

big blue pool in the lake. He slid over the ice and threw himself on his stomach to look into the clear water.

"I think I see some fish!" he shouted. "Maybe I could catch some for us."

"You'd freeze to the ice," Johnny warned him. "We all *work* up here—if only to keep warm."

Ashley proved helpful, and liked being part of the crew on men's work. At noon he lost his shyness, playing with little Joe.

"*Nee bah kah day,*" little Joe pleaded, pounding with his tin cup on the kitchen table.

"What kind of baby talk is that?" Ashley asked the small boy.

"That's not baby talk," Gerald said. "That's perfectly good Chippewa. It means, 'I'm hungry.' Indian Joe taught it to my little Joe—though I could have taught it to him myself. Come here to your father, Joe. *Wee wee bee tahn.*"

"Now *you're* talking baby talk," Timothy teased, hanging his cap on a nail.

"No, I'm not." Gerald laughed. "*Wee wee bee tahn* means 'Hurry up!' in Chippewa."

"Well, those are two handy sentences," Timothy mused. "I could get along fine in this life with 'I'm hungry' and 'Hurry up!' "

"Are you saying them to me?" Mary tossed a

smile over her shoulder. "Help me with this kettle, please."

Ashley sprang eagerly to help.

As he ate, he kept looking towards the frost-covered windows at the kitchen end of the cabin. They looked out on the river, but the curtain of frost was too thick to see through.

"So you like my frost pictures, too," Mary said, trying to draw Ashley into conversation. "They look like ferns and pine trees, don't they?"

As soon as Ashley had finished his pie, he walked to the window closest to the road, breathed a little space on it, and bent his head to look through this peephole. Then he rubbed at the glass with the warm heel of his hand to enlarge his view. Little Joe pulled at his trouser leg; he wanted to see out, too.

Billy said briskly, "Come on, everybody! If we all work hard these next few hours, we can finish the Burkhardt ice and start in on the smaller chunks for the Wilsons and the Murgners."

Soon Ashley was at work beside Timothy at one end of a crosscut saw. The boys, used to the resistance of heavy wood, whizzed through the huge ice block that Gerald and Billy had dragged onto the ice after sawing it and floating it in the open water. Whenever Timothy paused to rest, Ashley would squint down the river in the direction of Reads Landing.

"Expecting someone?" Timothy inquired.

Ashley answered Timothy's question with another. "Do you think the path along the river is safe?"

"You mean the path *on* the river?" Timothy asked. "I guess it is. It's good for snowshoe travel. The Indians use it right along, and so do the trappers. Mother won't let us walk on it because she's afraid of air holes."

"Would a horse break through?" Ashley persisted.

"Might," Timothy guessed. "But why worry? You haven't got a horse."

Laughing, Ashley bent to the singing saw again. He liked the queer, high tune of its cleavage. The winter sun flashed on the broad blade. So engrossed did he become that he failed to notice the sledge drawn by a single horse that was approaching on the river. Not until Billy yelled, "Ash! Tim! Come help!" did Ashley drop his end of the saw to rush with Timothy down the brush-laden snow onto the river smoothness.

Once at the base of the bank, they paused, breathless, for just a moment. In that instant they saw what was happening. The horse had broken through the surface ice and was sinking in the icy water. It was apparent that his struggles would soon carry the sledge, a wagon-box on runners, with him. On the blanketed seat sat two frightened boys. They kept sawing the reins, both grabbing and yelling and swearing.

"Jump out!" Billy's voice cracked like a whip. Then, as he drew near the struggling horse, he waded into the crackling ice, saying gently, "Whoa, Prince, old fellow. Take it easy. Ea-sy now."

He reached for the bridle, and, as he did so, sank to the shafts. Gerald came running along the shore with a plank that had been used in loading the ice, and Timothy and Ashley rushed to help him. Johnny Sterling waded out and got hold of the reins. He knew more about horses than any of them. The boys from the sledge splashed and scrambled to the shore.

"I can touch bottom," Billy reported, "but it's plenty cold. Got to get Prince out without breaking his legs or cutting them on the ice."

"Step here, Billy," Johnny Sterling called out. "There you are. Not that way! So! Steady, Prince. Steady!"

With the reins in his hands Johnny Sterling waded to shore. His hands were firm on the reins and Prince recognized that authoritative pull. Billy was struggling and so was Prince, but not aimlessly. Johnny directed every movement.

Gerald, with the help of Timothy and Ashley, got the wide, heavy plank into the water and held it firmly enough so that Billy could step up on it.

He pulled the horse after him, and although Prince snorted with fright he got his forefeet on the plank.

And now everybody but Johnny Sterling, who was still holding the reins, grabbed at harness and shafts and brought the horse safely to land.

"Here!" Billy shouted to Ashley. "Get a blanket and put it over the horse."

"We'll take him up to the house and give him a rub-down," said Gerald.

He led him along the shore, drawing the sledge along the stony, snow-covered path.

"Hurry, Billy!" Johnny Sterling warned. "Your pants are already frozen stiff, and if you don't get out of those boots you'll have chilblains all your life."

Timothy and Ashley were left to face the two boys who had caused all the trouble. They were the Flints!

"I don't know whether Ash expected you or not," Timothy said, "but you're not welcome."

"I did half expect them," Ashley admitted, misery in his eyes. "Mr. Murgner has been insisting they should come. He handled some otter hides for them a while back, and they didn't have the money to pay for the tanning. So he said they should come and take it out in work when he needed ice."

"That's right," Jake agreed virtuously. "Zizzy and

I came right along to Reads Landing to pay our bill."

"I'm sure Mr. Murgner sent you with Prince by the regular road," said Ashley. "Why did you take the river path?"

"Because it was shorter," Jake answered promptly. "How was I supposed to know it would be wetter?"

He guffawed, and Zizzy's squealing laughter applauded him.

"You haven't any sense," Ashley cried.

"That's a nice way to talk to your cousins, Ash," Jake whined. "Fine welcome you're giving us. Come on, Zizzy. We promised Uncle Max we'd get that ice and we're going to get it."

On Sanborn's Point Gerald had rubbed Prince down and covered him with a blanket. Mary came out of the house with some hot mash. Billy, in warm, dry clothes, was back on the job with Johnny Sterling.

The Flints, not at all abashed by their dubious welcome, dried themselves out in the Ferguson kitchen.

They soon appeared on the ice, offering to load the Murgner sledge box. Billy, who was always mild, consented to let them work. Work was good for anybody, he believed. But he insisted that Ashley drive Prince back to Reads Landing.

"All right," Jake agreed, "suit yourself. By the

way," he added, "did you ever find those muskrat pelts your brother accused us of taking?"

"No," said Billy.

"You run into kinda hard luck, don't you?" Jake sneered. "The big Ferguson cache wasn't as big as you thought, eh? Fergusons going to move back into their haunted house?"

"That's their business," Billy snapped.

"Come on, Jake." Zizzy tugged at his brother's sleeve. "I'm cold. Leave 'em be."

CHAPTER 14.

Timothy Gets an Inkling

BILLY WALKED UP THE HILL between Timothy and Johnny Sterling in the winter twilight after delivering the last load of ice at the Burkhardt icehouse.

"B-r-r-r!" He shivered. "Funny I didn't get warmed up helping to unhitch the horses inside the barn. I've got chills!"

"No wonder," said Johnny. "You were in that ice water up to your waist."

"Nonsense!" Billy shrugged. "I got right into warm clothes—though I must admit Gerald's woolens are worn pretty thin."

Billy had nothing more to say. He kept lagging behind, and when he reached the Dustin kitchen he sank down in a chair without taking off his jacket.

Isabel, stirring a pan of stewed tomatoes ready to set on the back of the stove, glanced up. "What's the matter, Billy?"

"Just tired," Billy answered. "Had a hard day."

"He got a ducking," Timothy explained and added hastily, at Billy's warning look, "But he got into warm clothes right away."

"Water never hurt anybody," Johnny Sterling said lightly, "though I never did rightly care for cold baths."

Mrs. Dustin came in from the sitting room, walked over to Billy, and laid her firm, cool fingers on his forehead.

"Get out of your clothes and into your sleeping woolens," she said. "Then come down to the sitting room and I'll have a cup of primrose tea steeped for you."

"I'm not sick, Ma," Billy objected, but his protest was feeble.

Half an hour later he was lying on the couch in the sitting room, bolstered by pillows and wrapped in warm blankets. Rella sat down on a stool beside him.

"Does the primrose tea make you feel better?" she asked.

"Naturally." Billy grinned at her. "Mother's primrose tea will cure anything that's the matter with you. You ought to know that."

"Anyway, I helped gather the plants this year," Rella said. "The rains made them very tall, and every stalk was full of yellow blossoms at the top, like China silk. The leaves were so clean that Mother dried most of it just as we brought it home."

Captain Dustin stamped in. He was all for sending to Wabasha for old Doctor Lincoln, but Mrs.

Dustin said she guessed she could handle a simple case of chills and fever—as indeed she could. She supplied the village with herbs she had gathered. Some of her knowledge had been handed down to her by her mother, some of it had been gleaned from Indian Joe, and some of it had been studied out from Dr. Gunn's book on medicinal herbs. Her stand-by was primrose tea and it worked miracles of recovery.

As the evening wore on, Billy began to feel much better. By Mary and Rella's bedtime, he had fallen into a deep sleep.

Timothy, settling into the feather beds upstairs that he usually shared with Billy, soon felt a warmth stealing over him. January was at an end at last. The Hard Moon was no more. He loved February with its promise of spring.

He must have fallen asleep at once.

It seemed like the middle of the night when someone shook his shoulder. He sat up, blinking, in the cold room, lighted only by the moon.

"Billy!" He recognized his brother. "Are you worse?"

"Sh!" Billy warned. "Get into your clothes and come downstairs. I want to talk to you."

"In the middle of the night?" Timothy complained, but Billy had already gone downstairs. Timothy heard him stirring up the fire.

His teeth chattering, he got into his clothes. But when he joined Billy beside the fire, warmth surged through him.

"There's somebody in the Ferguson house," Billy said at once. "Whoever it is feels safe, with the village asleep. If I hadn't been sick and gotten that first rest of the night, I wouldn't be awake myself right now. Wish I felt equal to getting dressed, but I'm still a bit groggy. Guess you'll have to do the job of investigating."

"I'll go right down there," Timothy said.

"There's a lighted candle that's been moving about—looks like a ghost, only I don't believe in ghosts." Billy sat forward. "The basement windows are boarded, and the most likely way in would be the summer kitchen window. Take Johnny Sterling with you."

"I can manage alone," Timothy protested.

"Take Johnny Sterling with you," Billy commanded.

"All right then," Timothy agreed reluctantly. "Only I'll probably rouse the whole house getting him awake."

"You'd better not take guns!" Billy was certainly giving orders. "A gun might go off and hurt somebody."

"What am I going to use?" Timothy demanded.

"Whatever is in the house will have to be handled

with fists, I imagine. But don't fight unless you have to. Looters are cowards. If they're caught, they'll probably turn and run. Now hurry up!"

Timothy went back upstairs. He shook Johnny Sterling awake, whispering, "I'm going on ahead to the Ferguson house. Meet me there?"

Johnny Sterling muttered a reply, and Timothy rushed back through the sitting room, explaining to Billy that Johnny would follow him.

In the coldness of the moonlit winter night Timothy ran down the hill. Billy was right. Someone was in the back part of the Ferguson house, on the ground floor, a candle flickering in his hand as he moved about.

Timothy rushed ahead through the sheltering brush, then moved more cautiously as he came near the house.

Billy had guessed right. The summer kitchen window was propped up with a stick. Timothy climbed in quietly, but he dropped to the floor with a thump.

"What was that?" Jake Flint's familiar voice rang out in the silent house.

"I g-g-guess the window slammed down," Zizzy said.

Timothy, lying as still as a shadow on the kitchen floor, watched Jake as he came back to the kitchen from the dining room, his hand shading the candle.

He stood still, listening. He could not have been in the house very long, because the candle was scarcely burned down at all. Billy must have been watching when he lit it.

Timothy held his breath.

Now Jake was crossing the kitchen to the big pantry and lifting the trap door that led down into the cellar. Zizzy took the candle while Jake fastened the door back with hook and staple.

Then Jake took the candle again, urging Zizzy down ahead of him.

Listening to each step as they descended, Timothy could feel the pound-pound of his heart. He began to inch himself over to the yawning opening that was dimly lit by the candle in the cellar. He dared not trust himself to walk for fear his steps on the creaking old boards should prove a warning.

Now his eyes were used to the feeble light. As he reached the trap door, he rose and carefully slid the hook out of the staple. Then he let the door fall with a resounding bang. It fairly shook the house. The Flints were trapped!

Jake let out a yelp of alarm, and Zizzy screeched, "I dropped the candle!"

"Shut up!" Jake shouted, and Timothy could hear the resounding whack he gave Zizzy, who bawled like a calf.

"Who's there?" Jake yelled.

Timothy did not answer. He heard Jake swearing as he felt his way up the cellar steps. Timothy stood on the door. When Jake found that he could not lift it, he shouted, "Get off that door, or I'll shoot."

Timothy did not believe that he had a gun, but there was no sense in taking chances.

"All right. Come up!" Timothy ordered.

"Oh, it's only you," Jake said, with unflattering relief.

"Hands up when you get to the top!" Timothy ordered, tightening up. "Get out of this house the way you got in!"

"We haven't taken a thing," Jake grumbled as he emerged.

"We didn't have time," Zizzy explained. "Don't tell me to shut up, Jake. Tim knows we didn't have time."

"Time for what?" Timothy demanded, but neither boy answered him. "This is your second try at stealing in this house. What are you after this time?"

"Don't you wish you knew!" Zizzy taunted.

"Listen, Dustin." Jake stood for a moment in the pantry doorway, hands above his head, trying to discover in the gloom whether Timothy carried a weapon. "I've got as much right in this house as you have."

"Sure," Timothy agreed. "Nobody has any right

in this house but the Fergusons. I'm not staying and you're not either. March!"

Growling, Jake lifted Zizzy through the summer kitchen window and climbed out after him. As Timothy stepped through the window, Jake whirled about. Now he could see that Timothy was not armed. He made a sudden lunge, grabbing Timothy by the legs. Taken by surprise, Timothy went down and the two boys became a mass of flying legs and arms. In the tussle, Timothy tried to free his right arm for the telling blow Billy had taught him. But Jake was bigger and heavier, and he knelt on Timothy's chest. Timothy could not breathe. He felt himself getting weaker, but he could hear Jake ordering Zizzy to start running.

The younger boy hesitated, and said, "Have we gotta go back without 'em again?"

Suddenly Timothy felt the weight of Jake's body lifted from his chest. In the gray light before dawn he saw the running figures of the Flint boys and then, turning around, discovered why they had fled. Johnny Sterling was coming along the path. Timothy got to his feet before Johnny reached him, and greeted him with the story of what had happened.

They walked back up the hill together. The snow was now pink with sunrise.

"Guess I dozed off again after you waked me,"

Johnny apologized. "Billy came up and got me going—thought you might need me."

"I needed you all right," Timothy admitted ruefully. "Guess I need more boxing lessons, too. But, Johnny, do you know what I heard Zizzy say? 'We gotta go back again without 'em!'"

Johnny gave a long-drawn-out whistle.

"That gives us an inkling of the reason for the Flints' interest in the Ferguson house," Timothy went on. "Jake may not have been looting or even planning to loot. Something he and Zizzy stole may be cached there."

"Well," declared Johnny, "we'd better ask Sheriff George Young to keep his eye on the Ferguson house from now on."

◇◇◇◇◇◇◇
◇◇◇◇◇◇◇

On a day of melting snow, late in February, the Dustins were surprised one evening, as they sat about the sitting room stove, by visitors—Henri Derosia and his father.

The elder Derosia had come to see Billy about his beaver peltries, which he wanted to buy. Richards Gordon, the St. Paul furrier, had agreed to make an overcoat for him.

The young people took over the kitchen, while their elders visited in the sitting room. Isabel and

Johnny Sterling had already started molasses taffy, and Mary and Rella began to pop corn.

Timothy said, "Come on, Henri, and help."

Henri was in high spirits. He paused in the sitting room doorway long enough to ask Captain Dustin if he would not give him a job on the *Johnny Smoker*.

"I'd like to help paint her this spring," he offered.

Captain Dustin stiffened a little.

"I may not paint the *Johnny Smoker* this spring," he said, after a moment's hesitation. "But if you can help build a barge, I can use you."

"Now, William," Mrs. Dustin chided, "don't tease. You know very well that you always paint boats in the spring. Everybody does. You may want to use Henri on something else, but that doesn't mean that you're not going to paint the *Johnny Smoker*."

"I'm afraid it does, Permelia," the Captain said, and his look said that he chose not to argue the matter.

Amazement was written large on Mrs. Dustin's face. Something was amiss. She would talk the matter over when they were alone. Most certainly her husband would paint the *Johnny Smoker;* he'd never neglect anything so important.

In the kitchen Henri relayed the puzzling news.

"Don't you worry," Isabel said pleasantly. "Father just naturally will paint the *Johnny Smoker* this spring."

"But he said he wasn't going to," Henri reminded her.

"Father's very amusing," Isabel explained. "He can pretend to be serious when he's fairly chuckling inside."

"He didn't appear to me to be chuckling," said Henri.

He forgot his perplexity as he watched the Dustins. The heavy syrup, congealing on the buttered platters, was soon ready to be lifted off and pulled. It looked so easy, the rope-like strands growing lighter and thicker as Isabel and Johnny teased the candy into lengths by tossing it from one hand to the other and drawing it out.

At last Isabel was twisting hers, and as she dangled the strand over a platter, she cut it into pieces with kitchen shears.

"I wish I might try," Henri said. "I've popped corn before, but I never made taffy—real pull candy like that."

"Johnny, give him a piece," Isabel directed. "Here! Let me cut him a bit. Rub butter into your palms, Henri."

Henri did as Isabel instructed, then accepted the piece of taffy that Isabel had snipped from Johnny's long strand. He was amazed at its softness. His warm hands made it melt still more, and when he tried to pull it from one hand to the other it stuck to his fingers. Rella and Mary sat down on the kitchen chairs to laugh. Johnny Sterling, in his amusement, could hardly manage his own candy.

Mr. Derosia came to the kitchen door to find out what was happening, the Captain behind him. Their roars of laughter brought Mrs. Dustin from upstairs, where she had been putting away linens she and Isabel had ironed that afternoon. She had wanted to give the men a chance to visit alone. Maybe, she thought, the Captain would explain to Mr. Derosia why he had joked the way he did about painting the *Johnny Smoker*—or rather about *not* painting the *Johnny Smoker*.

Henri was not dismayed over the sticky mess he could not manage. "Scrape it off for me, Isabel," he begged. "Let me wash my hands and try again. I can learn anything that anybody else can learn."

Isabel scraped off the taffy and Henri washed his hands in the kitchen basin and dried them well. Then he buttered his hands again and started in. This time the candy did not stick quite so much. But Henri had to get rid of the soft strands again and make a third attempt. This time he succeeded even to the extent of twisting the strands. Isabel cut it for him, and Rella and Mary did the sampling.

"Don't you and your sister ever make taffy?" Isabel inquired.

"No," Henri answered. "But if you'll give me your receipt, I'll teach her."

After the Derosias had gone, the Captain said, "Permelia, I like the spirit of young Henri." He stood beside the kitchen table and picked up a chewy piece of the candy Henri had pulled. "What was it he said? 'I can learn anything that anybody else can learn.'"

"Then, Father, why wouldn't you give him the job of helping paint the *Johnny Smoker* in the spring?" Timothy inquired. "We'll need a lot of extra help for that."

The Captain looked around the table at the family faces. The children were still sampling the popcorn and Mrs. Dustin and Johnny were clearing things away.

"I've tried to make it clear to all of you," he said, "that I am *not* painting the *Johnny Smoker* this spring. Somehow you just don't seem to comprehend it."

Their astonished faces told the Captain that indeed they did not.

CHAPTER 15.

Plenty of Paint for a Barge

◆◆◆◆◆◆◆◆◆◆◆◆◆◆◆◆◆◆

RELLA CAUGHT UP WITH Walter Richards on his way to a wood lot on one of his father's farms on the ridge. She marched along beside him as far as the schoolhouse. In time to their steps, he recited:

> *"Cold, frosty morning,*
> *Feeling mighty good.*
> *Ax on my shoulder,*
> *Off to the wood."*

It had become quite a ceremony with the two of them.

"Good-by, woodsman!" Rella shouted, as she turned into the school path. "Cut plenty of wood for the *Johnny Smoker*."

"I will," Walter promised, and his long legs increased his steps. "Nice green hickory and oak."

Funny, thought Rella, to call the wood green when there was not a leaf on a tree or even a swelling bud. But March was spring by the calendar, and the wind that blew over the snow certainly had a different smell because of its wanderings. Somewhere it must have touched warm, wind-swept hills with blooming crocuses.

Last year at this time Captain Dustin and a corps of helpers had been busy painting the *Johnny Smoker* a gleaming white. Last year he had even gilded the letters of the boat's name. Last year he and the boys had scrubbed every inch of the decks and had whitewashed the hull.

The school bell was ringing. Rella dared not loiter, but her thoughts ran along like a turbulent little creek in a rocky ravine. This year the Captain was building a barge, quite a good-sized barge, it is true, but not big enough to excuse neglect of the *Johnny Smoker*.

Billy and Johnny Sterling worked on the barge every single day, even though Pierre and Mr. Murgner and others did a good deal of the carpentry. After school Timothy and Ashley sawed boards already marked by Pierre. The boys all talked *barge* and all thought *boat*.

Mary and Rella could think of nothing else.

"It's like having a woodshed painted instead of a house," Mary grumbled to Rella, as the little girls raked the yard one cold spring Saturday afternoon, "to have that barge painted instead of the boat."

Rella jerked her rake through the tangled grass.

"Well, we're getting the back yard done first," she said, "so we can start the vegetable garden. The front yard can wait. Maybe that's the way with Father. He thinks the barge is more important to have ready first than the boat."

"You're finding excuses. The barge was done a week ago," Mary reminded her. "Instead of leaving it as it is, Father is even having a green trim put on it."

"I know it," Rella acknowledged. "Funny he won't tell us *why* he isn't painting the boat."

But if Mary and Rella were perturbed, Timothy was more so. As he worked on the green trim for the barge, a puttery job, he grumbled, "Plenty of paint for a barge but not enough for a boat."

Billy, working beside his brother, defended the Captain.

"You've got to trust Father's decision," he said. "He thinks as much of the *Johnny Smoker* as we do."

"Guess he does," Timothy conceded. "He can't be hard up, can he?"

"Some folks are saying he is," Billy answered dryly. "But we seem to have as much to eat as most folks."

It did not make sense.

The barge was scarcely finished before the hauling of the green wood cut by the Richards boys had to be attended to. Captain Dustin rented Mr. Burkhardt's team and wagon, and all during spring vacation Timothy and Ashley loaded green cordwood on the hill, brought it down the road to the levee, and piled it up to dry for river boat fuel.

The new freight cars that delivered goods at the back of Duerre's store only slightly dismayed the rivermen. They made comical, dour faces at the railway or shook their fists good-naturedly at the locomotive engineers who waved gaily to housewives and children. Yet the railway *was* competition; and, when Knapp, Stout, and Company began to ship general merchandise and to receive it by freight at a time when the boats were tied up waiting for Lake Pepin to open, the Captain openly expressed his worry.

"If I'd had any idea of the extent of the railway freight business, I'd have hated to build that barge," he confessed one night at supper. "We need it now and I thought it would be useful later."

The Dustin children kept their eyes on their plates, as did Johnny Sterling. People were saying that the Captain was getting "notional," not painting his boat.

"Now, William," Mrs. Dustin chided, "that's no way to talk. You know as well as I do that you wouldn't be building a barge if you didn't need it. It's going to be mighty handy to have extra wood for the *Johnny Smoker* right alongside—and plenty of space for extra freight."

The Captain gave his wife a mournful glance.

"The country's building up," she heartened him. "Reads Landing's got a dozen hotels now. But you can't get a piece of beefsteak around six o'clock when the raftsmen come in, nor a jug of molasses. It's a good thing I do my own baking. Louie Troutman's wife keeps busy just making those little sponge cakes and gingerbread cupcakes, and Louie himself works such long hours at bread and doughnuts that he can hardly take time off for meals. Railways don't go through towns that aren't prosperous."

It was seldom that Mrs. Dustin made long speeches, but she knew that the Captain needed bolstering, as usual, in early spring.

◇◇◇◇◇◇◇
◇◇◇◇◇◇◇

Now the sun shone warm on the hills. The day came when Mary and Rella burst into the house with their first crocuses. They had found them on a warm, sheltered hillside even though the snow still lay deep in the gully below. Mrs. Dustin set them in a soup plate of water. Crocuses were her favorite flowers. She loved the furry stems and calyxes, the pale, purple-blue petals like spring sky, and the gold centers like the sun.

The river had long since turned a dark color as the snow melted and the river ice began to show small ponds and shallow pools. A warm rain, with a strong wind, broke up the ice and started it down the river, but Lake Pepin remained frozen solid. Only in the river did ice pile up along the shores, then sweep into the current.

One cold, windy morning, while the Dustins were at breakfast, a deep, booming whistle broke into their talk.

"A packet!" Mrs. Dustin exclaimed.

She stood at the window, the coffeepot in her hands.

One and all, the family rushed into the yard, snowy and muddy except for the green grass near the pump.

It was indeed a packet, a shining white side-wheeler coming up the river on the far side of the island from Wabasha. It hugged the Wisconsin shore.

Shading her eyes with her hands, Rella shouted, "It's the *Savannah!*"

"You can't see the name from here," Mary objected. "Why doesn't she come over to the Minnesota side?"

"She's probably been fighting river ice all the way up from Iowa," the Captain said cheerfully. "When the rivers break up, there's plenty of business ahead. Look at the Chippewa ice rushing out ahead of that packet. Yes, Rella, it's the *Savannah.*

No telling when she'll get through the lake, but the longer Lake Pepin holds out, the better for Reads Landing business."

Billy squinted at the packet edging into position. "The *Savannah* may be the first through the lake this year," he said. "That Wisconsin shore is deep and sure. No matter! The *Johnny Smoker* was the first last year."

After the arrival of the *Savannah,* it was not many days before other packets appeared—the *Clinton,* the *Alexander Mitchell,* the *St. Paul,* and the *Dubuque.* By the end of a week, a dozen boats had sought shelter from the river ice in coves and sloughs. Roustabouts were kept busy with their pike poles, pushing the larger chunks away from the boats.

There was a growing impatience among crews waiting for the ice to go out of Lake Pepin so that the boats could get on up to St. Paul. Such delays meant loss to the owners in wages, fuel, and freight jobs.

But their loss was Reads Landing's gain. In addition to the added business, there was exciting entertainment. In the evenings there was music by the Negro orchestras. Cabin boys, cook's helpers, and roustabouts put on white coats at night and became singers and players. The villagers were invited on board for dancing and card parties.

Isabel, in her wine-colored cashmere, the ruffled polonaise trimmed with narrow black velvet, made a picture, especially when she wore Grandmother Houghton's gold and garnet earrings in her small ears. Johnny Sterling looked very handsome in the dark blue wool suit that had been made by Anton Lammers, the little old tailor who walked down to the levee every evening for exercise, after sitting cross-legged all day long.

Mary and Rella once visited the *Dubuque* with Isabel and Johnny. They were allowed to stay all evening and listen to the Negro orchestra. Always afterward, whenever they saw a Negro, they thought of melody and lights and laughter.

The older people often dined on the boats. The men played games, such as checkers and chess, or took bets on when the lake would open. Day and night the levees swarmed with roustabouts. Once in a while there were passengers fashionable enough to belong to another world, especially the fur traders who were on their way to St. Paul.

There was not a single boat that did not appear resplendent beside the *Johnny Smoker*. She was tied up on the Minnesota side of the river near the base of the island where the ice would go past her. Some packets in the most vulnerable positions kept crews on duty day and night, their pike poles ever ready to shove aside the ice that threatened to make knife-like jabs in their hulls. The *Johnny Smoker* remained serene—and safe.

The shabby little boat became the butt of much ridicule.

One of the loafers in Duerre's accosted Billy with the question, "When you big boys agoin' to get up enough gumption to paint your papa's boat? She don't look like no race-winnin' boat this spring."

"The *Johnny Smoker*," Billy said good-naturedly, "can beat any boat of her size on this river, with or without paint."

"Looks like she's goin' to have to without'n paint," the loafer persisted. "You boys hev got it perty soft this spring. Livin' on what the *Johnny Smoker* done last spring."

"You must have bet against her," Billy declared, and the other loafers guffawed.

Timothy could not take the teasing so blithely.

"Cap and you boys restin' up fer the summer's work?" a half-drunken roustabout remarked to him on the boardwalk of Richards Street one bright day. "Cap got bees in his bonnet, eh?"

"My father knows what he's doing," Timothy retorted, "and don't you forget it."

"They's folks that differ," the man said with a smirk. "They's folks think he's plumb daffy."

Timothy's fist shot out, but the roustabout bounded up like a rubber ball. He struck Timothy on the jaw with a right uppercut, and he followed the blow by blackening the boy's eye. Then he swaggered away.

Johnny Sterling bound up the eye with raw beefsteak, and the little girls wept; but Timothy refused to confess the cause of the quarrel.

"You ought to know better than to argue with a drunk, no matter what he says," Billy scolded.

"Don't I know it!" Timothy agreed.

His spirits lifted when he was called upon to do paying errands for the traders, among them a young business man from St. Louis. After a successful fishing trip, the trader said, "You deserve a special favor, Timothy. What can I do for you?"

"If you'd really like to do something," Timothy said eagerly, "maybe you'd turn over some of your freight to the *Johnny Smoker,* my father's boat."

"I don't seem to place it." The trader strode up the steps to the Union House, Timothy at his heels with the fishing tackle. "Jot the name down." He got out his notebook at the desk, then scowled at the name Timothy had written large and plain. "The *Johnny Smoker.* Oh, yes. Little side-wheeler at the island."

Timothy could feel the sudden reserve in his manner.

"She's a right good boat, sir," he assured the trader.

"You mean she *was* a right good boat," the trader corrected, then put his hand on Timothy's shoulder. "I was only joking. Didn't mean to hurt your feelings. And of course I'll keep my promise. She might not look so seedy, son, if she was painted."

Timothy repeated the conversation at home after supper as he and his father sat in the sitting room while the women of the family did dishes in the kitchen. Billy and Johnny were busy bringing in wood.

"Why do we have to take a back seat?" he demanded. "The *Johnny Smoker* would look as fine as any of them if she was painted."

"That's so," agreed the Captain, but he would say nothing more. He was as aggravating as the stubborn Pepin ice. He would move only when the time was ripe—if ever.

The April rains began, the buds swelled, the woods filled with Mayflowers and bloodroots and violets, and the wild plum blossoms were sweet on the roadsides. On clear days after school and on Saturdays, children swarmed up into the hills. And still the Pepin Lake ice held.

Ashley was busy helping Mr. Murgner cut wood on a small lot he owned, and Timothy wandered lonely through the woods. He had no wish to meet the jeers of the loafers and roustabouts regarding the shiftlessness of the Dustins. Knowing his temper, they took particular delight in teasing him. The latest jests hinged on the fact that the Dustins had a right fancy barge.

Moving like an Indian through the woods one day after a rain, Timothy saw otter at play, the young sliding down a mud bank. Then he discovered the fine trail of an ermine, and finally he followed a mother mink home to discover a baby mink, soft as a kitten and lovely as sable. That night after supper, when he told his father of his discoveries, he said he had a good mind to become a trapper on the way up to becoming a furrier.

"Always do your boasting at home," Captain Dustin advised. "The fur business, Tim, is the only business I know that can't stand advertising. I never yet knew a trapper that had a good year. If he admitted it, he'd have a run on his trapping grounds that would put him out of business."

"I can see that, sir," Timothy assured his father, feeling grown-up and immensely serious. "But a boat business is best advertised, isn't it? Look at the business the *Johnny Smoker* got after winning the race."

"No man likes to make a poor mouth," the Captain said. "If he does, he has a reason."

Timothy knew there was no further use in prying.

CHAPTER 16.

The Johnny Smoker Turns Back

◆◆◆◆◆◆◆◆◆◆◆◆◆◆◆◆◆

THE RIVER GLEAMED through the bare trees, its water dancing with pieces of broken ice. But the lake was still a solid expanse of ice which barred the impatient boats. Steam was up every morning now, and the piles of cordwood on the shore dwindled. Crews stayed for the most part on board, expectant; at any moment they hoped for the word that would send them on their delayed journey.

During the last week in April, there were showers, followed by sunshine. Now the oldtimers knew that it was only a matter of hours before the lake should open. Yet the *Johnny Smoker* was not ready for departure. From a dozen or more boats smoke curled back in great plumes, but the *Johnny Smoker,* still tied up at the levee, was not yet fully loaded, though the Dustin boys and Johnny Sterling had been carrying wood into the engine room until it overflowed onto the forecastle. A number of boxes of freight went on board, but it was plain that Captain Dustin expected more cargo.

A group gathered on the levee when the boys

began to load the barge with cordwood. It was evident that once he did start up to St. Paul, Captain Dustin had no intention of having to land to take on wood. Gradually the watching group was augmented by loafers until there was quite a crowd. Here and there some old friend of the Dustins stopped for a moment to stare quizzically through his pipe smoke at the Captain, puttering with Timothy over the roping of the barge to the wheelhouse.

One of them paused to inquire, "What's got into Cap'n, fussing over that barge like an old hen over one chick?"

"Don't wanta lose it!" a roustabout shouted. "By gar, I don't blame him. He'd do better to lose the boat!"

"That *Johnny Smoker* warn't sech a bargain arter all," a riverman decided. "Like a hoss that wins one race and is winded for keeps."

"Cap'n's kinda queer about the *Johnny Smoker*, sentimental-like," a raftsman said. "Mebbe on account she won a race. But he ain't aimin' to win another race, that's plain."

"Hard up, or he'd 'a' painted her," the riverman reasoned. "But I like the way his chin whiskers stick out, like he still had some fight in him."

Through the crowd rushed Indian Joe. For days' he had sat lazily on the deck of the *Johnny Smoker* or on the empty barge, with his gun across his knees. Now he was like a whirlwind, shoving the roustabouts aside with the butt of his rifle.

"Mr. Murgner coming!" he shouted. "Make way!"

He attracted so much attention that more and more people joined the onlookers. What was going on here anyway?

Presently Max Murgner, with Emma and Ashley on the seat beside him, rattled up to the gangplank that had been run out from the boat. He backed the wagon around, pulling on Prince's reins. The wagon box was piled high with bales. Here was the cargo the *Johnny Smoker* had been waiting for.

Indian Joe stood beside the wagon with his gun. His eyes never left the bales as Mr. Murgner and Ashley carried them up on the deck of the *Johnny Smoker*, where Captain Dustin checked them.

Then Billy and Timothy jumped down onto the barge, and Ashley and Johnny Sterling lifted down the bales to them, one at a time, to be stored in the center, with wood piled high on either side.

"Ho, ho!" a loafer shouted. "The great Ferguson cache, right out in the open where a skiff could snatch it off!"

"Do tell," his crony agreed. "Cap'n Dustin's gone crazy as a loon."

Another delay occurred while the Captain took

the tanner aside. Then Mr. Murgner came down the gangplank, looking immensely serious.

"Big business with the Cap'n, Max?" a neighbor inquired.

"Big business, you betcha," another neighbor agreed. "Max jumped on it like a duck on a June bug."

To the Reads Landing people, it looked as though Captain Dustin had a cargo for St. Paul after all. What it was concerned only the Captain himself.

◆◆◆◆◆◆◆
◆◆◆◆◆◆◆

On May Day the Dustins, sleeping quietly in their house on the hill while Indian Joe guarded the boat and barge, were awakened towards dawn by the crackling of shore ice. It was followed by a roar like the thunder of a mountain torrent. Captain Dustin's voice boomed through the house, waking everybody.

"Ice going out of Pepin!"

All over the village lights came on in the houses, and men, hastily getting into clothes and buttoning mackinaws as they ran, poured out of the houses. Mary and Rella, in bed, heard the shouts of the men using their pike poles to keep the great chunks of ice in the current and away from the boats, and they shivered deliciously. Mrs. Dustin even permitted them to get up for a few moments in the unheated bedroom, to look out of the window. Then she hurried them down to the kitchen to dress.

Mountains of churning ice were rushing out of the lake into the river, filling the channel with up-ended blocks and surrounding the boats that often blocked the flow of ice until the shouting roustabouts pushed the chunks aside with their pike poles.

After breakfast every able-bodied person in Reads Landing was down on the levee. Many of the packets had to back downstream with the current because of the ice jam, before they could make a start up through the lake to St. Paul.

Steam was up on the *Johnny Smoker*. The Captain and the boys were on board. Like the others, they had backed a short distance downstream to avoid the worst of the ice.

Now the stage was in, drawing up in front of Duerre's store. The moment it stopped a boy fairly tumbled out.

"Captain Dustin!" he shouted. "Where can I find Captain Dustin?"

Mary and Rella rushed up to him with squeals of delight.

"Henri!" they shouted. "Henri Derosia!"

Their words tumbled over one another, asking

questions, for Henri looked as if he were full of news.

"I have a message for your father," Henri explained hurriedly. "He must have it before he starts for St. Paul."

His glance followed the little girls' pointing fingers. He saw the *Johnny Smoker* struggling in the grinding, churning ice with her freshly painted barge lashed fore and aft.

"But I've got to get this message to Captain Dustin," he cried desperately. "I've got to!"

From an inner pocket he drew forth a letter, sealed with red wax. Running down to the levee, he waved it wildly.

"Come back, Captain Dustin!" he yelled. "Come back! Come back!"

In the midst of the noise of bells, whistles, and orders being shouted from the boats fighting the ice, Henri's voice was just another shout.

Mary and Rella rushed after him, one on either side, grabbing his arms.

"He won't come back," Mary cried.

"He can't come back," Rella added.

"What'll I *do?*" The letter was shaking in Henri's hand as he asked the question.

"Go out to the boat," Mary ordered.

"How?" Henri inquired wildly.

"In a skiff," Rella explained. "Our boys always catch up to Father in a skiff if they're late."

Max Murgner, the tanner, watching the progress of the *Johnny Smoker* with Ashley from his wagon seat, got down and walked over to see what the trouble was when he saw Henri's hand with the letter in it waving above the crowd. He called Pierre and explained matters, calming the distracted Henri at the same time.

"Sure I catch the boat. Never you mind," Pierre promised. "Henri, you are big, strong boy. You help me rowing, eh?"

Henri was relieved to be able to get into action.

In a few moments Pierre had launched his skiff. He handled one pair of oars. Henri on the seat behind him, handled the second pair. Ashley, leaving Prince's reins in Emma's hands, rushed down to the levee, borrowed a pike pole from one of the rivermen, and stepped into the prow of the skiff just as Mr. Murgner was shoving it off.

"Good idea, Ashley." Mr. Murgner praised his nephew. "If you can be of help to Captain Dustin, go on board."

Even with Ashley vigorously shoving ice cakes aside as they collided with the skiff, it made slow progress. Already the *Johnny Smoker* and the other steamers were plowing out into the lake where the water was more open.

Mary and Rella began running along the shore, waving and calling to their father. They had often run along the sandy path beneath the frowning bluffs. Always before their father had waved at them from the pilothouse.

But today Captain Dustin seemed absorbed in his fight to keep the boat in the channel. The little girls ran swiftly; they were so used to the river path that they did not even stumble. If only they could call their father's attention to the skiff struggling in the ice jam!

"Father, please wave!" Rella begged.

The little girls had rounded the curve of the shore in front of Sanborn's Point before the Captain saw them. The Point was a landmark. Gaily he waved from the pilothouse window.

Instead of waving back, Mary and Rella pointed to the skiff. The Captain looked back and saw what they were pointing at. He blew the mellow whistle of the *Johnny Smoker* to let his little daughters know he understood, and the boat swung around as he headed back towards Reads Landing and the skiff.

Out on the wide lake, the skiff made slow but certain headway. Most of the boats, both side-wheelers and stern-wheelers, had long since gone up the lake. Even the slowest ones now passed the *Johnny Smoker*, leaving trails of foam that splashed

up about her. In the bright May sunshine the boats looked dazzling white on the blue water. There was very little surface ice in the lake; most of it had been swept into the river channel.

The *Johnny Smoker,* her engines idling, awaited the arrival of the skiff. Captain Dustin turned over the wheel to Billy and was on the lower deck when the skiff came alongside the barge. Indian Joe, sitting on a bale, his gun beside him, reached for the landing rope. Pierre snubbed the skiff against the barge with an oar, and Henri and Ashley clambered up over the heaped bales and wood, still panting from their efforts. Timothy gave them a hand onto the deck of the boat. Johnny Sterling remained in the engine room, and Pierre waited quietly in the skiff.

Captain Dustin took the letter from Henri, broke the seal, and read it quickly. His jaw set, his chin whiskers lifted, his blue eyes blazed.

"What is it, Father?" Timothy begged.

"It's a letter from my father—from the Dousman house," Henri offered. "It's very important. I thought I'd never get it in your hands, Captain Dustin. I tell you I feel relieved."

"Go back and tell your father you delivered it, Henri," Captain Dustin commanded. "Thank him for me. Get going."

"How about me, Captain Dustin?" Ashley inquired. "Mr. Murgner said if you needed me, I was to stay."

"Stay," Captain Dustin ordered. "We'll need help."

As soon as Henri was back in the skiff the Captain rang the bell for all steam ahead. By the time Pierre had shoved off with Henri, the *Johnny Smoker* was kicking up twin waves of foam.

◇◇◇◇◇◇◇
◇◇◇◇◇◇◇

In the pilothouse Captain Dustin took the wheel from Billy. After a while Billy clattered down the steps and rushed into the engine room, to send Johnny Sterling up. In a few minutes Johnny came out of the pilothouse and shouted to Timothy that his father wanted to talk to him.

Timothy slammed the pilothouse door with a loud bang as he went in, taking the tall stool beside his father's.

"Father, what is it?" he demanded. "What did you tell Billy and Johnny? They're all on fire with excitement. What was in the Dousman house letter?"

Captain Dustin spoke bluntly. "The Dousman scouts have information that we are to be attacked by fur thieves. Possibly tonight. It is suggested that we keep with the other boats, the big ones going to St. Paul, for protection."

"We can never catch up with them," Timothy exclaimed.

"We must do our best," Captain Dustin said grimly. "The entire Ferguson cache is on board the *Johnny Smoker.*"

"Out on that barge?" Timothy was so indignant that he yelled. "Why, it would be the easiest thing in the world to snatch it off."

"Young man," said the Captain indignantly, "listen to me. I said the entire Ferguson cache is on board the *Johnny Smoker.* It has been on board since Max Murgner and I brought it down here one snowy night last winter. It is in the hold."

"Then what are the bales on the barge?"

"Mostly hay, son," the Captain answered, smiling.

Timothy was silent for a moment. Then the bewilderment disappeared from his face. "I understand," he exclaimed. "The reason you didn't have the *Johnny Smoker* cleaned up and painted is because too many people would have known about the cache being on board. And you didn't think we could keep our mouths shut."

"Good reasoning," observed the Captain dryly, his eyes squinting at a landmark ahead.

"Does Indian Joe know?" Timothy inquired.

"By instinct," Captain Dustin replied. "He may

not have a proper bump of location. Seems to be guarding the bales on the barge with his life."

"Father, I'm worried." Timothy jumped to his feet. "We don't seem to be catching up with the big boats. Do you think we can?"

"We could if the wind stayed in the east," the Captain said.

"But it's veering around to the north," Timothy pointed out. "We're bucking it. See that water, and listen to the engines throb."

Timothy went back down to the engine room to help the boys. All afternoon the three of them fed the insatiable, wood-burning firebox. The wood that had been piled in the engine room was gone by afternoon, and by sunset the wood on the lower deck was practically used up.

"We're going to need the cordwood on the barge," Billy observed. "I'll speak to Father about it."

After a talk with his father in the pilothouse he returned to the engine room.

"Get busy, Tim," he cried, "and come and help me. Father wants us to bring all the wood on the barge over onto the deck of the boat. He says to distribute it evenly."

"What a job!" Timothy grumbled, but he leaped lightly onto the barge and was soon lifting the cordwood up to Billy.

Twilight gave way to darkness. The boys ate

snacks at their posts. The *Johnny Smoker's* plumes of smoke rose higher and thicker.

Captain Dustin called down to Indian Joe, "Come on board, Joe."

Grumbling, Indian Joe obeyed. Was this the time to leave the barge unprotected?

CHAPTER 17.

Attack on the River

◇◇◇◇◇◇◇◇◇◇◇◇◇◇◇◇◇◇

CAPTAIN DUSTIN had called Indian Joe on board only to give him instructions. He was to take Ashley on the barge with him but was not to fire at all unless any possible attackers succeeded in boarding the *Johnny Smoker*.

"Make a show of resistance on the barge," Captain Dustin instructed. "Do not risk your own life. No matter how tempted you are, Joe, remember that capturing these fur thieves alive will help your country more than anything else."

Indian Joe grunted his disapproval, but he did not argue.

The *Johnny Smoker* plowed through the growing darkness with all her might. She left Red Wing behind, keeping in the middle of the river current.

The river looked black and cold as all the light faded. The engines throbbed like the heart of a racer. The Captain's instructions had been for all steam ahead and he did not change his orders. He rang no bells and gave no hint of his uneasiness.

All night long the gallant little steamer strove

to catch up with the bigger boats heading for St. Paul. But she had been too long delayed in the lake, the wind had blown too strongly from the north, and the dwindling fuel had to be conserved. The Captain no longer dared to run the boat at top speed.

The *Johnny Smoker* had almost reached Prescott when a skiff shot suddenly out of a slough ahead of them. Such boats were not unusual, for many sportsmen started out at break of day. The sky was beginning to grow pink in the east. The lanterns of early milkers going to their barns looked misty.

As the *Johnny Smoker* passed Prescott, the skiff moved closer and closer. Billy, rushing up to the pilothouse, cried, "Father, they're trying to edge you over onto a sandbar. Either they're drunk or they don't know the river."

"They know the river all right, or they wouldn't know where the sandbar is," Captain Dustin snapped. "Go below, and remember my instructions. Stay with Johnny at the entrance to the hold, your guns ready. Let Timothy tend the firebox. Let Indian Joe and Ashley take care of the barge. No matter what happens, do not leave your posts."

"Yes, sir," said Billy.

The *Johnny Smoker* did not slow down nor did she speed up. She maintained the right of way. Her warning whistle ordered the big skiff out of the channel, and seemingly the warning was obeyed. The skiff moved away, but as the big boat came alongside, swept back against the barge.

The men who were rowing kept their places, but two agile fellows wearing handkerchief masks leaped up from under the blankets in the bottom of the boat. In their right hands were gleaming knives. As they boarded the barge and ran for the ropes that made it fast to the boat, Indian Joe made a flying leap to the deck of the *Johnny Smoker.* With the butt of his rifle, he cracked down on the hands of the first man. Too late! The man, having cut through the ropes, dropped down among the bales. It would have been easy to shoot him. It took all Indian Joe's will power to remember Captain Dustin's orders.

At the back of the barge Ashley made a running leap at the second man, whose knife was raised to cut the ropes that bound the barge aft. But even as he jumped the man, the long blade cut the ropes. Then it fell from his fingers, and he and Ashley rolled over and over into the bales. The barge drifted away from the boat. There was no help for it. The barge was gone and Ashley was a prisoner.

The *Johnny Smoker* had no choice but to go on to St. Paul, leaving Ashley, for the time being, to his fate.

As the boat docked at the wharves of the city, a

policeman observed, "The *Johnny Smoker!* The smaller and shabbier they are, the more noise they make. A cordon of us sent down here to guard that boat! Well, maybe somebody important is on board."

As Timothy slid out the gangplank and Billy ran with the landing rope, a distinguished-looking gentleman got out of a waiting carriage.

"Mr. Gordon!" Timothy exclaimed, hurrying down the gangplank. "I'll tell my father."

"Your father knows I'm here," Mr. Gordon said, following Timothy on board. "In fact, I'm here at his request. Well, Timothy, we seem to be pretty deep in the fur business."

"I hope so, sir," Timothy said. "But the barge was stolen, and we're much concerned over the fate of my friend, Ashley Flint."

"The barge was stolen? Good!" Mr. Gordon cried. "It will be picked up and your young friend rescued. The Dousman people notified us of the renewed activity of this fur ring, and government boats were in hiding, just waiting for that skiff to make a haul. Not only will Captain Dustin get his cargo back—I understand it is mostly hay and hides—but, more important and much more remunerative, he will receive a reward for the help he gave in capturing the thieves."

Captain Dustin came down from the pilothouse to greet his guest.

"I have the entire Ferguson cache on board, Mr. Gordon," he announced proudly. "The seals and threads have been identified by Mr. Derosia of the Dousman house, with whom the bales were registered. Mr. Murgner and I put the twenty-four bales on the *Johnny Smoker* one snowy night. They are in the hold. They have accumulated dust and dirt, but in this seeming neglect there has been the most careful watchfulness."

The two men shook hands. Timothy, standing beside his father, felt a rush of tenderness and understanding. His father had endured jeers and blame to guard the Ferguson treasure. Even his own sons had doubted his wisdom.

A half dozen men in plain business suits came up the gangplank and were introduced to Captain Dustin by Mr. Gordon.

"These men are under bond," Mr. Gordon explained. "With the help of a police escort they will take the twenty-four bales up to the store."

"Follow me," Captain Dustin said quietly.

He led the way to the hold, where Indian Joe, with Johnny Sterling, guarded the bales.

"Is he under bond?" Mr. Gordon inquired, indicating Indian Joe.

"I'd say yes," Captain Dustin answered and

touched the Indian's collar of blue and white wampum edged with wildcat's claws.

"I understand," Mr. Gordon said with a friendly smile. "Mr. Derosia wrote me that this fine Indian saved Gerald Ferguson long ago and helped to raise him."

Indian Joe gave an embarrassed grunt. He was glad to see Billy and Johnny Sterling walk in so that Mr. Gordon's attention was directed to them.

"Even my family did not know my plan," Captain Dustin explained to Mr. Gordon. "I felt that the responsibility should rest on me alone, since it was my idea to let the searchlight fall on the barge and away from the shabby boat. I did tell my boys and Johnny after we left Reads yesterday morning, because I didn't want them to risk their lives to save the bales on the barge."

One by one the bales were lifted out of the hold by Indian Joe and the three boys. Then the bales were transferred to carriages. Timothy rode in one, Billy in another, and Johnny Sterling in a third. The last two bales, with the special pitch seals and the colored threads, were loaded into a hack; Captain Dustin rode inside with Mr. Gordon, and Indian Joe on the seat beside the driver.

In the Gordon Fur Company's carefully guarded room the bales were unpacked. Timothy's eyes smarted, his mouth quivered, and his heart beat

high. If men used to beautiful fur gasped in aston-
ishment, it was not strange that the boy should be
so touched. It was a dream come true—furs soft as
veiled clouds, furs luminous as silver, more beautiful than golden light, deep brown as sunlit leaves
in autumn, black and silky as midnight, and all
treated by some process that had kept them lovely
through the years.

Even in his joy Timothy had not forgotten Ashley.
Mr. Gordon was not a man to make idle chatter. He
had said that the government men would attend to
everything. But suppose Ashley were badly hurt!
His father assured him that the men were fur thieves,
not murderers, and they would have no reason to
hurt Ashley.

It was with a thrill of relief that Timothy saw a
vigorous young officer admitted to the guarded
room.

"We got them, sir," the officer greeted Mr. Gordon. "All four of them! They had abandoned the
skiff when they saw us and had scattered into the
woods near Prescott. We hunted them out and
took them at the point of our guns."

"How about the barge?" Captain Dustin inquired.

"We'll get back your barge, sir, never fear," the
officer promised Captain Dustin.

"But Ashley!" Timothy pressed forward. "My

friend, Ashley Flint, was on that barge. He attacked one of the thieves. Did you find him?"

"I'm sorry," the officer apologized. "Our first concern was, of course, the capture of the fur thieves. They had moved the bales from the barge into various skiffs that had been waiting in the sloughs. But our men were so swift and so hot on the trail that the skiffs were abandoned. The bales are in the police station; the Chief says they contain mostly hay and hides, he believes. Of course his examination was not thorough."

"It was thorough enough," Captain Dustin said dryly.

"Father! Mr. Gordon!" Timothy was white. "Please explain to the officer how important it is to find Ashley. We've got to find him. Please, sir, may I go with you?"

"Very well," the officer agreed, at a gesture from Mr. Gordon. "Our opinion is that the young man probably got ashore and will come in to the city. He could get a lift almost anywhere, now that all the farmers are coming in with milk and eggs. We'll continue our search, however."

Timothy accompanied the officer to a small government dock. On the shore near by were several horses, saddled.

"Can you ride?" the young officer inquired.

"I've never ridden much," Timothy admitted, "but I can manage."

The mists were cold, rolling in from the river. The officer led the way on a big gray horse; Timothy followed on a little brown mare. The officer led the way to farmhouses to make inquiry. No one had seen a boy who answered Timothy's description of Ashley.

"Perhaps your friend would try to stay near the barge," the officer suggested. "If he's the kind you say, he'd want to guard it. It's right down this way; the government men will bring it in to the wharf later in the morning."

The searchers rode along the shore.

"This is the place," the officer said. "I remember that clump of willows. But the barge is gone! What could have happened to it?"

"If it wasn't carefully drawn up on the sand," Timothy reasoned, "it may have drifted into the current, blown by the wind. I know which way the current would take it from here."

"Then *you* lead the way," the officer directed.

Timothy, unused to horses, was saddle-weary by the time he reached a curve in the river channel that ran close to the shore. A cove with tall trees jutted out, and the wind at this point often drove boats landward. Timothy's heart suddenly lifted. There lay the barge, rising and falling on the waves like an immense cradle. A familiar tarpaulin had been thrown over something in the bottom. The bales, however, were gone, just as the officer had said.

Timothy slid off his horse and slipped down the embankment. He waded out to the barge and climbed over into it. As he ripped back the partially fastened tarpaulin, he uttered a cry that brought the officer to the river's edge.

"Ashley!" Timothy shouted in relief. "It's Ashley! Wait a minute, Ash. I'll help you."

Ashley Flint had been tied and gagged, and he lay, scarcely moving, on the bottom of the barge.

"Don't try to talk, Ash," Timothy begged, "until I get you a drink and fix you up."

But once Ashley was freed of his bonds, his words overflowed in a torrent. "Gone! All gone! All the bales gone! I can never face the Fergusons. I should have fought harder. I did my best. Then I tried to get away and get help. They caught me and put me back in the barge and tied me up."

Hastily Timothy explained that the bales were safe. He told the story of the Ferguson cache being hidden on the *Johnny Smoker*. Ashley sniffled a little as he said, "Good old *Johnny Smoker!*" Then seeing the officer's gaze on him, he calmed down. His arms about Timothy, he rode back to the government wharf on the brown mare.

A little later Ashley had told his story to the police officers. With Timothy and Billy he walked over to the Merchants Hotel, where Johnny Sterling was waiting.

As the boys sat down to their noon dinner, Billy said, with a twinkle much like Captain Dustin's, "Maybe I shouldn't mention it in the same breath with the Ferguson cache, but I wonder what became of my sixty muskrat skins."

CHAPTER 18.

The Fergusons Come Home

◆◇◆◇◆◇◆◇◆◇◆◇◆◇◆◇◆◇◆

IT WAS AMAZING, said everybody in Reads Landing, how Mrs. Dustin could find room in that salt-box house on the hill for so much company. But the Dustins never objected to doubling up or setting on a few extra plates. Besides their own family and Johnny Sterling, the Dustins had the Fergusons and Henri Derosia as guests.

The entire value of the Ferguson cache had not as yet been estimated, but even a partial appraisal assured the Fergusons of a handsome sum. The household was in a sparkling mood.

"You look fatter already, Gerald," Mary observed, as she passed him the crab apple jelly at supper time the first night that the young couple came in to talk things over with the Captain. "But what shall we do for ghosts? For years the place has been called the Haunted House. I can hardly realize that it's really going to be our home."

"If you want a ghost," Rella offered eagerly, "I'll be glad to haunt it."

"You're too small," Timothy objected. "Ghosts

should make long, black shadows, such as Henri or I could make. Or Johnny."

"How about me?" Billy inquired. "I'd like to cast a shadow. Have you all forgotten that I have a cache somewhere belonging to me? Or aren't sixty muskrat peltries important compared to silver fox and ermine?"

"Your muskrat peltries *are* important, Billy," Mary Ferguson said gently. "We should help you find them."

"Shucks!" Billy said, and looked embarrassed. "They're not important, but I can't help being curious as to what became of them."

"One thing you can be certain of," Timothy declared, "is that they won't be stored in a nice dry cave in cedar."

Everybody agreed, and now Mrs. Dustin shooed the diners into the sitting room.

"Father, shall you be tied up at the Landing to-morrow," Timothy asked, "or do you have to take out a load of freight?"

"With no crew?" The Captain lifted his chin whiskers so that his beard stuck straight out. "No, sir. I'm turning you all over to Gerald for tomorrow, so that the Fergusons can get a good start on the sea of prosperity."

"Lake Pepin's good enough for me," said Gerald

in the doorway beside Henri, "with such neighbors as you Dustins."

"Count the Dousman house in, too," Henri said. "We'd like to co-operate."

"Want to co-operate on a saw, Henri?" Timothy inquired. "The Haunted House is still damp and cold. Mother suggests we saw some stove lengths to be handy tomorrow morning."

"Let's get going," Henri agreed. "Guess we can see by the light from the kitchen. That's a fine kerosene lamp."

◆◆◆◆◆◆◆
◆◆◆◆◆◆◆

In the morning, after an early breakfast, the young men from the Dustin house started downhill to make the Ferguson house comfortable enough for the women to work in. Mamie Rand was at the Dustins' early, to take over the small children so that Rella and Mary could be free to run errands for Mrs. Ferguson and Isabel, who would be busy hanging curtains and rearranging furniture.

Striding down the hill, Billy and Johnny Sterling led the way with scythes and axes. Timothy, Henri, and Gerald followed close on their heels.

"Suppose we start with the basement," Billy called over his shoulder, "taking off the boards and letting some sunshine into the place!"

"Good idea," Gerald agreed. "By the way, I saw those Flint youngsters hanging around again early this morning when I went to pump your mother a pail of water. I understand that the Dousman men put Jake and Zizzy in the custody of the Murgners —but they were to be turned over to Sheriff Young in case of trouble. Their cousin—what's his name— was with them."

"Ashley," Timothy informed Gerald and added loyally, "He's a friend of mine."

"Yes, Ashley," Gerald said. "Too bad so fine a chap has to have those young scoundrels about. They worry him, I imagine."

The workers left the hill road and waded down through the weeds that surrounded the Ferguson house. The sheriff came to meet them.

"Knowing you folks were moving in today and might have doors open or windows pried up," he explained, "I came right over. Saw Jake and Zizzy wander over this way after young Ashley left them, to haul something for Max Murgner. If they're round about, I guess I scared 'em away, so they won't bother you folks."

"Thank you, Sheriff," Gerald said.

While Timothy and Henri cut weeds, Billy and Johnny began to pry the boards from the basement windows, straightening the nails as they came out and chopping the wood into kindling. Gerald brought out the carpets to be cleaned.

Johnny found an old broom in the summer kitchen and began to sweep away the accumulated dirt and leaves around the base of the windows. He rubbed away the winter soil with some old rags Mrs. Dustin had insisted he take along.

Timothy left his pile of weeds to make a suggestion. "I'll go down and unlock the windows from the inside," he offered.

"All right," Billy agreed. "What with the melted snow and spring rains, these boards certainly stick."

Timothy lifted the trap door in the pantry and felt his way down the basement steps. He was too hurried to bother with candle or lantern. He thought he heard a scratching, scurrying sound as he reached the bottom step, and he made a mental note to lend the Dustin cat, Africa, to the Fergusons. As Rella said, "Where Africa goes, no rat grows."

Groping his way across the damp, dusty floor, he looked about for something to climb up on. At first the dimness confused him so that he almost got onto a broken chair. Then he saw a packing box of about the right height. He reached over to shove it under the window closest to the stairway.

Then he became aware of heavy breathing. A shiver ran along his spine. It might be an animal, a bear perhaps. Timothy backed away. Now there

came an audible whimper from beyond the packing box and then a choking sound.

"Come out of there!" Timothy's mouth was dry,
his voice hoarse.

Nothing stirred.

"Come out or I'll come in after you," Timothy
threatened.

The cellar was very still.

"You can't hide for long. The house is surrounded."

Still no sound!

He took hold of the packing box and pushed it
around. As he did so, one end came loose and he
stepped on something soft, then something that
crackled. But he had no time to investigate. He
jumped up on the packing box as if to reach for the
window catch. If he pretended to turn his back, he
might tempt his enemy out of hiding.

That was exactly what happened. He heard a
rush of stumbling feet, and just as the dark figure
was about to tackle him from behind, he flashed
about and fell forward on his attacker, knocking
him to the stone floor with a force that sounded as
though he had cracked his enemy's skull. But Jake
was very much alive—for Timothy knew at once
that it was Jake—and he squirmed and kicked.
Timothy had all the advantage, however, and his
fists pummeled the face of the big fellow under

him until they began to feel sticky with the blood that oozed from Jake's nose.

Zizzy, seeing his brother losing a battle, screeched at the top of his lungs. His screams brought Billy and Johnny Sterling stumbling down the steps, followed by Henri and by Gerald with a lantern.

"What's going on here?" everybody shouted at once.

Gerald lifted the lantern and the scene became clear.

"Get up, Tim," Billy said sharply. "Can't you see you've knocked him out?"

"So it's Jake again!" Johnny Sterling cried. "How did you get in, fellow? The sheriff said he was around until we arrived."

"The sheriff came and we couldn't get out," Zizzy explained. "Then all of you came just as he was leaving, and we still couldn't get out."

Jake rose groggily to his feet. He kept mopping at his nose with an already bloody handkerchief.

"You won't none of you believe me," Jake said with a convulsive sigh, "but I was going to give Billy back his muskrat peltries. The Murgners have been good to me, and I don't want to get into any more trouble." He collapsed on the bottom cellar step, his head in his hands, and groaned.

"It's true, what he says," Zizzy hastened to explain. "Jake was going to put the muskrat pelts back in the Dustin woodshed. We brought 'em down here on Emma Murgner's sled, but we were going to carry 'em back in a bale cover. See?" He dragged out a piece of canvas with attached roping.

"Just where are my peltries?" Billy demanded.

"Right there," said Zizzy, indicating the box that Timothy had pushed towards the window.

Now Gerald's lantern revealed the pelts that Timothy had stepped on. His shoes had broken several shingles.

Billy lifted one of the cone-shaped shingles that Timothy had brought him from the mill on that bright blue fall morning. Then he picked up another and another. He counted them out, all sixty of them.

"They've really been carefully packed," he said. "Jake, if you'd use your abilities the right way, you could make a good, honest living. Too bad we have to turn you over to the sheriff."

"Do we?" Timothy inquired. "Don't get the idea, any of you, that I'm soft. I'm not. But what I suggest is this: that Jake sign a confession of this theft. We'll hold it. Then if he does any more tricks, we'll turn the confession over to Sheriff George Young."

"That's fair enough," Jake said soberly.

"I'd like it that way," Gerald decided. "After all,

the Ferguson cache was discovered because you were looking for the Dustin cache."

◆◆◆◆◆◆◆
◆◆◆◆◆◆◆

The Ferguson house hummed with activity.

Below, the boats came and went on the shining blue Mississippi. Emma came up the hill with a bouquet of wild roses.

Timothy stood for a moment on the hillside out in the Ferguson yard, looking down at the *Johnny Smoker* tied to the piling. His smile expanded into a broad grin. There were three figures on deck, all busily wielding paintbrushes—the Captain, Mr. Murgner, and his friend, Ashley Flint. The sun brought out the gleaming whiteness of the new paint.

"Everything in its own time," Timothy remembered the Captain saying. This *was* the right time to paint the *Johnny Smoker* so that the little side-wheeler could carry proudly on.